DOCTOR
Heartbreak

A DOCTORS OF EASTPORT GENERAL NOVEL

D.M. DAVIS

www.dmckdavis.com
Cover Design by Thunderstruck Cover Designs
Cover Photo by Depositphotos
Editing by Tamara Mataya
Proofreading by Mountains Wanted Publishing & Indie Author Services
Formatting by Champagne Book Design

This book is a work of fiction. Names, characters, places, and incidents are either the product of the author's imagination or are used fictitiously.

This story contains mature themes, strong language, and sexual situations. It is intended for adult readers.

About This Book

D.M. Davis' *Doctor Heartbreak* is a second-chance, doctor-patient, heartbreaking romance of loss and unrealistic promises that threaten to keep Dani forever lonely and break the only organ Dr. Heartgrove doesn't know how to fix.

I'm intimately familiar with the brain, but it's the heart that's giving me trouble.

I found her in a bar.
Red hair and a rocking body teasing me with promises her eyes threaten to keep.
She marked me without saying a word.
Tattooed her name on my soul.
One night was all we had.
Come morning she was gone.

Eight months later, I find my redheaded temptress on my gurney, holding a little boy like he's her lifeline.
Turns out he's her nephew, and the only promises she's capable of keeping are those made to her dead sister.

We may have started out as a drunken romp, but I've no intention of letting that be all we are.
I want more than one night.
I want forever.

When Dani wakes up in the ER, the man of her fantasies staring down at her, can she find room for him among her family obligations, or will she run as fast as she can, living for others instead of herself?

Dedication

Have you ever had a one-night encounter and wished it had been more?

This is *more*.

DOCTOR
Heartbreak

One

"**H**ENRY, WHY DON'T YOU PUT YOUR BOOK DOWN and look at this amazing view?" I try to coax my sweet, brainy nephew to live in the moment instead of inside his newest passion—Harry Potter books.

"But,"—his gaze dashes to me, out the window and back to his book—"Hermione is getting ready to fix Harry Potter's glasses."

I rub his back, smiling. His excitement over every magical word as if it's the first time he's read them is too endearing to squelch. "What is this, your fifth or sixth read-through?" Even though he's cute as all get out doesn't mean I can't tease him a bit.

"Seventh." His wide smile, so much like his mother's, chips at my soul. "I keep telling you, Aunt Dee, each time I read it, I finds new details I missed. I want to read till I know it all by heart, till I'm right there with Harry, Ron, and Hermione. Till…" His words fall away, already lost in the pages.

I kiss the top of his strawberry-blond head. "I know, kiddo."

He's been through enough. We all have. As he escapes into the world of Hogwarts, I lean back and focus on the coastline of Eastport, Rhode Island, as it flashes by. The swoosh and click-clack of the train lull me into calm, and I allow myself to drift open-eyed, thinking of the beaches and all the fun we'll have once it warms up and we can spend our days playing in the water without freezing our heinies off.

It might possibly be our last summer together. Richard, my brother-in-law and Henry's father, is thinking of moving back to Pawtucket, where his restaurant is, when Henry starts kindergarten in the fall and I go back to school. I'll be sad to leave the town I grew up in, but they are my only tie here besides endless memories full of heartbreak I should be happy to leave behind.

Richard hasn't exactly asked, but he hasn't said he *doesn't* need me anymore. I'm not sure which will break my heart more: not seeing Henry every day, or knowing they no longer need me when I can't imagine my life without them.

Since his mother died, Henry is pretty much the only reason I get up every morning. He's the reason I smile and continue to put one foot in front of the other. Henry and Richard are my purpose, have been since the day everything changed.

The panic on Lucy's face has my fork suspended in air, but it's the screaming and shouting growing in the background like a carnival ride gone wrong that get me to my feet.

"Run!" she shouts. "He's got a gun!"

"What?!" Guns aren't allowed in hospitals. I move to look behind her, but she snags my arm, pulling me around the corner and through the double doors of the kitchen. "We can't be in here."

"Shh," she silences my protest and ridiculous reaction that we

aren't allowed in the kitchen. She grabs my arms, hugging me tight. "We'll be okay. Just stay down."

Gunshots ring out on the other side of the doors. People run around, in and out of the kitchen doors, their squeaking protest somehow comforting. Until a woman falls to the floor beside me.

There's a hole in her head.

"Ohmygod!" Lucy muffles her scream, her wide eyes flashing to me.

"We can't stay here." My brain finally working, I spot another exit and tug her toward it. Left should open into the corridor where we can escape through the loading dock, but right leads back to the cafeteria and danger.

Lucy runs in front of me, always the protective older sister.

"Go left," I whisper-yell seconds before she crashes into the hallway.

Bang. Bang. Bang.

I try to reverse course but only slide through the door, slamming into Lucy when two more shots ring out from down the hall.

I'm the reason my sister is dead. She was visiting me that day for our weekly lunch.

"Aunt Dee." Henry's nails dig into my arm as his grip tightens and he starts to shake it. "Something's wrong."

The familiar panic on his face—so much like his mom's—shoots me into high gear. "Pack up your stuff." I glance around; concerned gazes dash from face to face as more and more passengers begin to note... "We're slowing down." Fast. Too fast and nowhere near the station.

Out my window, around the curve, I spot another train. "Ohmygod." *Please, God, no. Not again. Don't let me get Henry killed too.*

We're going to crash. We need to switch seats. I pick him up and pivot us so we're sitting with our backs to the front of the train. "Press into the seatback." I lock my arm over him, gripping the opposite arm rest. "We're going to crash. We're going to be okay, Henry."

"I know." He pats my arm. "Mommy's looking out for us."

My sweet boy, I pray she is...

The jarring shaking and squeal of the brakes send my heart into fits and my mind into overdrive. *Please, please, take me. Save Henry.*

Take me. Save Henry.

Save Henry.

Save Henry.

Save Henry.

"It's okay, Auntie Dee, Mommy gots us."

The sound of his sweet, faithful decree is the last thing I hear before the roaring crunch of metal and screams fill the air.

It's hard to focus through the chaos.

I grip Henry to me, protecting his head. "It's okay." *It's okay. It's okay,* I repeat, unable to hear my own voice, but I keep saying it in case he can hear me, and keep praying in case *He* can hear me:

Save Henry.

Save Henry.

Please. Please. Please.

The roar grows deafeningly loud. The impact, finally hitting our car, slams us into our seatbacks.

So much pressure. Can't breathe.

Save Henry.

People, belongings become airborne; some fly past us; others crash into each other.

Can't breathe.

Save Henry.

Their faces... The screams.

I close my eyes.

Please, God, save Henry.

Suddenly, we're thrown forward, backlash from the impact.

I curl around Henry.

We slam into the other chairs and then the floor.

Henry whimpers, but I don't let him go. *Save Henry.*

Save Henry.

Save Henry.

Then… nothing.

Two

I WALK AWAY, AS I ALWAYS DO.

No, I'm not interested in having drinks or dinner... or babies with you.

No, I'm not having a quickie in the on-call room.

No, you can't suck me off.

No. No. Just... no.

They never learn. I don't encourage them. I barely look at them. What could it possibly be about me that has them coming back again and again when all I have for them is *no*?

Women baffle me.

I pursue. I will not be pursued.

There are plenty of men out there who like being dogged. I am not one of them.

Take the hint. If I were interested, you'd know without a doubt.

But in this case, I will never have an intimate relationship with anyone I work with ever again.

Ever.

I, unlike them, have learned my lesson.

Nadia was a mistake; my semi-regular hookup tried to bring me to my knees. She wanted more. I wanted out. She didn't like taking no for an answer. She couldn't believe having sex for months hadn't led to me wanting more. I told her in the beginning it was mutual gratification only, nothing more. I have no desire for more with her or anyone else...

Well, that's not entirely true. At the time I broke off things with Nadia it was true. Then I met *her*. She's the only woman who has ensnared me enough to consider a *forever after*. But I foolishly let her slip away in the middle of the night, with only her first name and her scent in my possession. I considered never changing my sheets again. Nearly.

Now, on a huff, Jackie exits the doctor's lounge, as if she had a right to be in here in the first place pushing her medical wares, coming in with her blouse unbuttoned till the top of her breasts were on display, thinking I'm a desperate, testosterone-driven male, seeking to nail every woman who steps in my path.

Hardly.

I have more self-control than that. I have standards. Self-respect.

The sense memory of my mystery woman has me stiffening and finishing off my coffee before I go down *that* rabbit hole.

Jackie's interest reminds me of the last time I felt anything for another woman. Damn, that was eight months ago.

My phone sounds with the familiar beep of the emergency trauma alert.

Train collision. All hands. 15 minutes out.

I scarf half of my tasteless sandwich, chuck what's left, and make a pit stop at the men's room. Who knows when I'll get another break.

It's controlled chaos when I step into the ER, the first wave of injured having arrived.

Nurse Sweet directs traffic like a proficient machine. She thrives in this environment. "Dr. Blake, Bay 1. Dr. Clements, Bay 7."

I wait. Antsy for my turn.

Nurse Sweet swivels and darts by the gurneys as they pass, checking her tablet, eyeing the ED, determining who can go where. Orders fly in all directions.

The doctors meet each gurney the EMTs continue to roll through the sliding glass doors, spewing patient stats in rapid fire. As a neurologist, I'm called to consult on multiple cases. Like most traumas, head injuries abound. We're eight beds in when my name is called by Nurse Sweet. Rushing over, I begin my assessment before laying eyes on the woman and child on the table, locked in a fierce embrace.

"We couldn't get them apart. She's out cold, but wouldn't let go—he's okay." The lead EMT advises. "Figured better to just bring them in together than risk further injury..."

He continues, but my focus is drawn to the little man blinking up at me. "Hey. I'm Dr. Heartgrove. What's your name?"

"Henry." His hoarse whisper alerts me of many potential factors: smoke inhalation, rough from screaming, crying, or he could simply have a cold. So many details still to be discovered.

"Henry, how old are you?"

"I'm five." He starts to hold up his hand but tightens his grip when he realizes he'd have to let go.

I'm not sure who's protecting who here. "Henry, we're going to take good care of you and your mom." For the first time, I take in the unconscious woman holding, protecting him to her very essence. I lift the bandage on her head, inspecting the large scalp laceration on her right parietal ridge. "Debridement and staples."

I move on to her face. My breath catches as all the air is

sucked out of the room. *Red hair*. I'd missed it with all the blood. I grip the bed. It can't be.

Dani.

"...My mom is dead."

My focus flies to the boy, zooming in on his words. "I'm sorry, what?"

He softly smiles, his intelligent eyes taking me in as I do the same. "This is my Aunt Dee."

Dee?

"My mom died when I was three."

"I'm so sorry, Henry."

His smile grows. "It's okay. She's here—" He touches his chest. "My daddy and Aunt Dee takes good care of me."

"I can see that. Henry, I need your help—"

"Okay."

"I need to examine your aunt. Do you think you could let go so I can do that?"

He nods. "Aunt Dee said we'd be okay. She protected me."

"Yes, and she did a good job." I slowly coax him to let go.

He looks up at his aunt. "But she hasn't woken up." His gaze returns to me. "You'll make her all betters, Dr. Heartgrove?"

"Yes, Henry. I'll do everything I can to make her better." I motion to the nurse across from me. "Nurse G is going to take good care of you while I take care of your aunt."

"G?" He scowls at me and then Nurse G.

She leans in close. "They call me Nurse G because most can't pronounce my last name."

"What is it?" Henry whispers as if it's a secret.

She smiles and whispers, "Giurgiovich."

"Gurgoveech?"

"Close. You can call me Nurse G or Nurse Diane. I answer to either."

"Okay, Nurse Diane." Henry settles on a name and relaxes into the gurney, his aunt still gripping him for dear life.

It takes some work, but I manage to loosen Dani's grip on her nephew. Once he's free, he holds out his hand for me to shake. "Promise you'll takes good care of her?"

I'm shocked at his maturity. Such a strong, brave young boy. He's five, wanting to shake on his aunt's care instead of crying in fear for what they've been through, or the fact that he's leaving the only person he knows… the person who probably saved his life today. I've seen grown men whimper at the sight of a needle; I doubt Henry would crack a sweat.

I firmly shake his hand, not hard, but hard enough for him to know I'm serious. "I promise."

Before he's wheeled out, I stop them. "Henry, what's your aunt's full name?" I know the nurse will get his details, but for the moment I need to know as much about Dani as I can, besides the fact she's stunning naked, likes mojitos, kisses like a nympho, and can rock my world in two seconds flat.

"Danielle Hurley. She likes to be called Dani, but Aunt Dee's my special name for her."

Danielle Hurley. Dani.

Wake up, baby, so we can officially meet.

Three

I T'S SLOW, THE PULSING IN MY HEAD ACCOMPANIED BY THE rising urgency that I need to *do* something, *be* somewhere, but I don't know where or what.

Henry. His name floats to the surface. His precious face comes into view. My little man.

Ohmygod. Henry!

"Save Henry," I barely manage.

"Henry is fine. Can you open your eyes, Dani?" Such a handsome voice. Is that even possible? Can a voice be handsome?

Sexy, maybe?

"Dani." A warm hand touches my face. "Can you hear me? Open your eyes, baby."

Baby?

Who would be calling me baby? No one, that's who. I like this dream.

I blink and squint at the blurry form before me. A face. Even in the fog, I can tell the sexy voice has a jaw crafted by the gods. "Henry?"

He smiles. "Henry is fine, Dani. Do you know where you are?"

I try to lift my arm to rub my eyes but groan at the effort. "Blurry." I blink a few more times.

"You probably have a concussion. Take your time."

His voice. So familiar. He reminds me of… "Flint?!" I nearly come off whatever it is I'm on.

Large hands gently push me back down. "Shh, don't try to sit up."

"How?" Did I hit my head?

The throbbing is answer enough.

"Am I dreaming?" I capture his face, blinking away the moisture, finally bringing him into focus. "Is it really you?"

His wide smile pushes on my palms before he turns his head and kisses my right wrist. There's a gasp in the room, but I'm too focused on the striking face before me. Dark hair, light brown eyes lined in dark lashes I'd give anything to have compared to my light ones. And those lips. God, I remember what those lips can do. How they taste. How they…

"Give us a minute," he speaks over his shoulder.

Whispered responses and shuffling feet fall away as his eyes return to me.

"It's me, Dani." He sits on the edge of the…

I glance at my surroundings as things slowly start to come back.

"You're in the emergency room. Do you remember what happened?"

"Train… We… Henry. Oh my God, where's Henry?!"

With gentle hands, he settles me again. "He's fine. He's with a nurse. Go easy, Dani. I don't want to sedate you. You've hurt your head, and I haven't had time to do a full exam. I need you to lie still until I can assess your injuries."

"Flint, I don't understand. How? You—"

His sweeps in and... Kisses me.

Ohmygod.

Tender. Gentle. Oh so gentle. "I'll explain if you give me a second, but you have to remain calm." He eyes the machine next to my bed.

"I'm not sure kissing me is the best way to keep me calm."

His soft chuckle has me smiling and wincing. "It's completely unprofessional too, but I couldn't help it. We've much to discuss about that night. But at this moment, I'm really happy to see you."

Oh, yes, *that* night. I'm more than happy to see him too.

"However, there are more pressing items we need to discuss. You and Henry were in a train wreck. Two trains collided. You hit your head and were brought into my ER unconscious."

"Your ER?"

"I'm a doctor, Dani, here at Eastport General."

I hooked up with a hot doctor and didn't even know it? I mean, I knew he was smart because we did talk between... But a doctor? *Focus.* "And Henry wasn't hurt?"

"You still had him wrapped in your arms. I practically had to pry him loose." He runs a finger down my cheek. "He's fine. A nurse is watching him until his dad arrives. You can see him as soon as I finish my exam."

I grip Flint's arm when he tries to stand. "You're sure Henry is okay? He doesn't have any internal injuries?"

"I'll make sure, Dani." He steps to the door and speaks to someone before he returns.

"Your brother-in-law is already here with Henry. Would you like to see him?"

"Um..." I move to touch my head, but Flint stops me.

"Probably best not to touch. You've got a pretty good-size gash I need to clean and stitch up."

"Do I look scary? I don't want to scare Henry or Richard. My sister died—"

"I'm sorry—"

"She was shot. I'm sure I look scary. I don't want to retraumatize them." I can't have them see me like this if it will only bring back Lucy's death. We've come so far—

"You're more beautiful than I remember." He fingers my hair before his warm gaze encompasses me. "I've looked for this hair and this face everywhere I go."

The yearning in his words makes me ache. I've looked for him too. Just not too hard. My life is a disaster, and yet so mundane that, quite possibly, the disaster is the reality that I have no life outside of Henry and Richard. No room for fleeting affairs that will only break what's left of my heart. I have to devote all I am to Henry and Richard. It's my fault they're without a mother and wife.

"I… Flint… I couldn't—"

"It's okay, Dani." He clears his throat and presses a button. "Let's get your exam underway and your head fixed up."

The moment the nurse enters the room, his demeanor stiffens. This must be his Doctor Flint persona. I only know Bedroom Flint, who was much like the version who greeted me when I awoke. I think I much prefer the latter to the former.

Four

"**T**HEY SUCKED YOU BACK IN, DIDN'T THEY?**" ROGER laughs as he stitches up our patient's leg.

"They didn't suck me in, Dr. Blake. I'm on the Trauma Team." Continuing my assessment to determine if there's a traumatic brain injury, I ignore any further ribbing from Roger. He's a good doctor and not a bad guy to relax with over a few beers.

Based on the patient's responses, I recommend a head CT to rule out anything greater than a concussion.

I leave the patient in Roger's hands and move to the next, doing what I can. My years as an ER doctor haven't gone to waste—I rarely need to call in a consult.

Then a woman comes in with a metal rod sticking out of her abdomen. I rule out head trauma and leave her to the specialists stepping in to lay out their plan of attack, as I do when a sustained injury is not in my wheelhouse.

"Dr. Heartgrove, Ms. Hurley is back from CT."

I stop at Barbara's news, nearly missing her quizzical

look—the same look I've received from others who witnessed my reaction to Dani. They don't understand. *She's* different. I can't explain it. I don't know why. I just know her pull on me is irresistible and constant.

"Thank you, Barbara. Do you know if the little boy she came in with is still here?"

Barb points through the double doors. "They didn't want to leave until they saw her."

I ask her to bring Henry and his father to Dani's bay as I slip in to check on her myself.

Her smile bowls me over. "I was afraid I wouldn't see you again."

I fight to stay professional when all I want to do is slip into bed with her, reassure her I'm not going anywhere, and hold her until *I'm* sure she's alright. Then love on her until I—and her—know she's mine. "How are you feeling?"

"Good." Her smile falters. "I mean, my head is throbbing, and nearly every inch of me hurts. But in light of surviving a train wreck, I'm doing pretty good."

I'm hit with the memory of her eternal optimism the night we met. Like me, she was drinking alone. She wasn't looking for company. She was sad, drinking to dull the pain, yet she still saw the good in every topic that came up. I was drinking to forget. I wasn't looking for company until I saw her. Then I couldn't think of anything else but taking her home, helping both of us forget everything except each other, even if only for a little while. Then waking up and doing it again and again.

But she ran off before we could be more than a one-night stand. I scared her, or she scared herself.

"I'm glad to hear it." I resist the urge to grab her hand as I move closer. "Your CT scan hasn't come back yet, but I'd like keep you overnight. You were unconscious for quite a while and pretty banged up with two bruised ribs. Your creatine levels are high, showing muscle breakdown from muscle fatigue."

"But I'll be okay, right?"

"Yes." I grip her hand momentarily, wanting it to be so much more. "You'll be fine. You're pretty banged up, but your head laceration will heal, and you'll have a nice war-story scar." It'll be hidden in her hair—next to the one she already has I've yet to ask her about.

A knock on the door has me stepping back as she says, "Come in."

Her little brave man comes running in, followed by who I assume is his father. "Whoa, slow down, Henry. Aunt Dee is hurt, remember?"

Henry comes to a skidding stop beside her bed. "You're okay, though, right?" His gaze slides to me. "Dr. Heartgrove promised he'd takes good care of you like you takes care of me."

"Did he?" Her canted head and quizzical brow have me nodding my agreement. I did promise, and I always keep my promises.

Smiling, Dani pats the bed, urging him up. I want to object because of her bruised ribs, but there's no stopping Dani from being sure Henry is unharmed—thanks to her.

I introduce myself to Richard as he eyes the two in the bed, letting out a shaky breath in relief at seeing she is, in fact, alright.

"She'll be fine," I assure him.

"Yeah." He nods and wipes at his eyes. "I was really scared. Driving over here—" He sniffs and clenches his jaw. "I could've lost them too."

I give what I hope is a comforting squeeze to his shoulder. "But you didn't. They survived. Henry hardly has a scratch. She protected him with her body." She was willing to give her life for his, I've no doubt.

"Can we go home now?" Henry asks his father.

"Uh—" Richard looks to Dani then me.

"I'd like to keep her overnight for observation, keep up the IV fluids, pain meds to give her the best start on healing."

With that news dropped, I step out, giving them time to visit.

I need to get her admitted and check on other patients.

Five

THEY MOVED ME TO A ROOM SURPRISINGLY FAST, CON-sidering how busy the ER was. I haven't heard back on my CT, but Flint said he'd check on me later. I hope he does. I'm still a little shocked to find him again in middle of such a terrifying event.

I was sure I'd never see anyone again when Henry and I bounced around the train car like a rubber ball, much less my dreamy hookup from eight months ago. I've dreamt of him, fantasized, and secretly hoped, but I never truly thought it would happen. I don't go anywhere if it's not with Henry. Bar hopping is out of the question and so not my style. I'm a fuzzy-slipper, yoga-pant, comfy-sweater, watch-a-movie-on-the-couch kind of girl.

He doesn't go unnoticed. He's oblivious or hides his reactions well. I don't blame the nurses and staff for their ogling. I can relate. Flint draws me in like the thirsty girl I am, dying to quench my hunger. He's a hottie with a capital HOT.

He's so much more though. You'd think being a nurse—in

my former life, before Lucy died—I'd recognize a doctor. I had no idea. He swept me up in his swoony voice, clever mouth, and decadent body. Only his eyes spoke louder than anything else. He was hurting. I was hurting. There were no details shared. Only first names and promises of what the next few hours would bring.

Blinding passion and utter bliss.

Repeatedly.

I press my hands to my burning cheeks, wantonly blushing from the memory of that night. It's been eight months, and I still throb with want and ache to ease the loss in his eyes when he looked at me as if he was as baffled by our incendiary connection as I was—am. It's still there. It may only be a pilot light, but I've no doubt if we fed it, we would combust.

A soft knock draws my attention to the entrance of my room where the man of my risqué thoughts stands, his frame filling the door the way his body did mine.

"Hey," my breathy welcome has me blushing further.

"May I come in?" So proper, a gentleman all of the sudden. Yet his question doesn't sound like a question at all.

"Do you usually ask your patients if you can enter their room?"

He locks on my reddened face, his brow quirking. I want to look away, but I can't. I've missed him, if that's even possible. Who knows if I'll get more than tonight with him. So, I'm soaking it all in—all of him he's willing to give—to tide me over until I break down again and seek physical comfort I can't get from Richard and Henry.

I promised Lucy I'd take care of her men, and I plan to. No matter I'm a second-hand replacement. I could never live up to the example Lucy set. She lived for Richard and Henry. They were her dream, her passion. Being a mother and wife was all she ever wanted. She went to college for the *what if*.

What if she never found the *one*?

What if she never had kids?

College was her back-up plan, her second string. For Lucy, this life with her men was her everything. I can never replace her, be her, love them like she would—did. But I'm dedicated to the task of taking care of them, no matter the cost.

Cost...

The man at the door is the cost. One of them. There are so many. Friends I gave up on after the shooting. Too afraid to relive the incident every time we spoke, or them asking about Henry and Richard. Did they approve? I don't know. I never gave them the chance to weigh in.

I jumped headlong into the deep, only coming up for breath once in the year since she died.

Flint. He had been my breath. My escape. My minute of grabbing something just for me, *only* for me, not shared, not selfless, no forethought, no plans, only feelings, passion, and greedy, greedy need.

I've dedicated my life to them. It's just sometimes... a girl needs *more*.

"Usually, I ask their parents."

"What?" Not the response I was expecting.

He pulls one of the two chairs closer but eyes the bed like he'd rather sit next to me as he did in the ER. "I'm a pediatric neurologist."

He says it like it's no big deal, like he bags groceries instead of saving the lives of children—or anyone, for that matter. The fact I've seen him naked is the only reason I'm not completely intimidated by the proof of his intelligence. "I think I'm a little old for you then."

He laughs as he pushes the chair back and sits on the edge of the bed, capturing my hand. "Actually, I'm the one who's a little old for you." The crinkles at the corners of his possessive brown eyes allude to his kindness. "But I'm also not your doctor. It didn't seem right considering—"

"We've had sex?"

"—our connection." He pauses when my words register. His soft gaze turns stern. "You and I both know it was more than sex, my little runner." Leaning in close enough to kiss, he studies my face, compassion and desire mixed in his stare. "It's palpable, Dani. Don't you feel it?"

I feel it *everywhere*. "Yes." I exhale more air than sound, fighting the urge to lick my lips—or his.

He nods, taking the last of my air with his scorching gaze before leaning back, the mask of Dr. Heartgrove slipping into place. "I have to finish rounds. I'll be back in a bit. Dr. Clements, who will oversee your care, should be in shortly to discuss your CT results, but I saw nothing troublesome. Don't worry."

I grip his hand as he stands to leave. "You'll be back?" So needy, I know. I just...

He's in my face in a flash. "Look at me, Dani." He tips my chin till our noses touch. "You and I may have only known each other for a night, but I promise you this: I wanted more than one night with you then, and I most definitely want more now." He seals his words with a toe-curling kiss that has me forgetting my injuries, baggage, and the truth that we can never be more than a few stolen nights.

But I'll take it, cherish every morsel, and relive them until the day I die.

Six

THE TRIAGE FROM THE TRAIN WRECK IS LONG OVER, patients either treated and sent home or checked in for further care. We were lucky. It could have been far worse. It's been hours, and Dani keeps seeping into my thoughts, pulling me to her, just as she did eight months ago.

I found her in a bar, sitting alone. I stole the seat next to her, practically growling at the guy who was trying to beat me to her side. Amber eyes flashed to mine, marking me without saying a word.

"Hi, I'm Flint. I'd like to buy your next drink." My larynx barely cooperated as I fought for control. *I can't mount her right here at the bar. Can I?*

She leaned in, lifting her sweet ivory hand in offering. "I'm Dani." She tattooed her name on my soul. "And I'd like that." Pink lips, red hair and a rocking body teased me with promises her eyes threatened to keep.

And just like that, I was done for. I didn't know it then. I felt it—my world listing to the side, coming off its axis—but I didn't comprehend the extent of her impact on me. The waves of her tsunami took a while to breech my consciousness.

One night was all we had.

Come morning she was gone.

All around me lay the remnants, proof of her existence, her impact, her power to rock my world. Physically. Existentially. Sheet, comforter, and blanket were strewn around the bed and floor. The mattress was half off the bed that was a few feet left of where we started. More clothes than I could wear in a week lay around the bedroom—I have no answer for that one.

At one point I wanted her to wear one of my shirts when we grabbed a snack to refuel. I don't remember it looking anything like this. But to be frank, she was my focus, my delicious snack right on the kitchen bar, taking my fill as she begged me to make her come, mewling how badly she needed it.

She was insatiable, like she was trying to cram a lifetime of sex—*live* a lifetime—in a single night. But it wasn't just sex. We had deep, life-affirming discussions between orgasms. Cuddled and made out like teenagers until we'd nearly combust. And then combust we did. Repeatedly.

My chest aches at the thought. Was that what she was doing—trying to live an entire lifetime with me in one amazing, fateful night?

Did she run *from* me and our connection or back *to* her life?

Are Henry and his dad her buoys or anchors?

Do they help her float or keep her down, tied to one place—to them?

I all but bark orders at the nurse looking at me with begging eyes and pouty lips. *No. Just no.* They never learn. It will *always* be *no*.

Wrapping up my last patient notes, I head to the doctors' lounge to grab my belongings. I've got a redheaded temptress to see. I promised her I'd be back. I keep my promises... especially to her.

Dr. Clements gives me a double take when I bump into him at the elevators. "Ah, Dr. Heartgrove, I wanted to let you know I've discharged Ms. Hurley. Her scan was clean, as I'm sure you're aware." His eyes return to his phone, where he's furiously typing.

"Repeat." I couldn't have heard him correctly. I specifically stated she needed to remain overnight for observation.

"I discharged her." He meets my steely gaze.

"She's concussed, has rib contusions, and a large parietal ridge laceration. I wanted her observed overnight." My ending words were harsher than the beginning. It can't be helped. He didn't follow my orders; though, in truth, he doesn't have to.

He clears his throat before squeaking out, "Then you should have kept her as your patient. We needed the bed." He begins to walk off, faster when I step in his direction. "Nice job on the staples, by the way."

Yeah, like that throwaway compliment makes it all better. "How long ago?" I holler after him.

Glancing at his watch, he replies, "Twenty minutes, tops," before disappearing around the corner.

Twenty minutes.

I flash to the elevator then to the stairwell. I run for the stairs, bound down the four stories, and hit the first-floor entrance at a jog, coming to a stop at the curb, where my little runner sits on a bench waiting... alone.

Hands on my hips, I take a breath, then two more until I can speak without sounding as if was chasing her, which of course I am. She doesn't need to know that. "You shouldn't be out here by yourself."

"Flint."

Her surprise at seeing me, possibly anyone, has me looking

around, trying to figure out what she's waiting on. "Is Henry's dad coming to pick you up?"

"No—"

"Good. Come with me." I offer my hand, wanting to give her a choice, when really, I want to pick her up and carry her to my car.

"What? Where?" Her head hesitates, but her hand lifting to mine conveys her trust.

"Is he expecting you?"

"Who?"

"Richard."

"Oh, no. I didn't want to bother him. They had a rough enough day as it is and just got home. I'm waiting for a cab the front desk called for me."

I pull her along, slowing my pace, remembering her injuries. "Well, I'm sure someone else will use it."

"Where are we going?"

I smile at her acceptance, her leaning into me. "Home." She nods, sinking further into my side as I slip my arm around her. "How's your head?"

"Pounding."

Steeling my reaction, I open the door for her and help her in. She silently watches as I buckle her seatbelt. I want to kiss her pouty lips, but first… "Food and Tylenol will help. Close your eyes. Rest." I kiss her cheek before rising. "I got you."

I close her in and stalk to the driver's door. She could have used a night of IV meds and morphine for the pain, helping her sleep instead of feeling every achy bump and bruise. Soup and a hot bath are first on the agenda.

She's asleep before I even hit the straightaway to home.

I wonder what she'll think when she realizes I didn't mean *her* home.

Seven

FLOATING. I AWAKE, WARM AND GROGGY, AND... FLOAT-
ing. For the second time today, I blink into the warm gaze
of the man from my fantasies.

"Hey." His voice is like warm slippers and fuzzy sweaters,
comforting, familiar, and safe.

"Hi." I glance around the familiar surroundings of his bedroom as he lays me in his bed and starts slipping off my shoes
and socks. How many times have I wished to be back here, back
in the only place I'd taken something for myself in the last year
and a half... "You brought me to the scene of the crime."

"The only crime that happened that night was your little
disappearing act." The hurt in his voice stings.

"Flint—"

He silences me with a gentle kiss. "My little runner." Another
kiss. "No sneaking out tonight. You need to rest."

His kisses say so much more than *rest* is on his mind, but his
glance at my head ensures that's all that'll be happening tonight.

"Soup and Tylenol," I remind him, gripping his hand as he

stands, my silent apology and promise to not run out on him again. At least not tonight. Henry and Richard think I'm staying the night at the hospital. There's no reason I can't steal another night with the man of my dreams. Just one more.

He smiles at the connection. "On it." He fluffs another pillow behind my head before moving to the bathroom, turning to face me at the last minute. "I'll start a bath if you feel up to it."

My aching body screams *yes*. "Sounds nice."

On a small nod, he slips inside, the water turning on a moment later. I fight to keep my eyes open, to not give in to the need for sleep. I know I'll feel better if I bathe and eat something before slipping into unconsciousness.

He finds me minutes later, struggling to sit up. "Tell you what." He grips my shoulders till I'm steady on the side of the bed. "Let me get the soup heating, then I'll come back and help you." He steps back, eyeing me. "Don't try to get up on your own. The water will automatically stop when it's at the right level."

Fancy. I nod and lie down. No reason to waste what energy I have sitting up doing nothing. I'll just rest my eyes until he's ready.

"Dani." With a warm press of lips to my cheek, his breath tickles my ear. "Wake up, baby. You need to take meds to help your head."

Slowly he comes into focus. I nod and try to sit up with no more success than my previous attempt, my ribs protesting, and my energy zapped. "I'm so sore."

"I know. These will help." He drops some pills in my hand. "It's just Tylenol. I don't have anything stronger. If you need it, I can have Dr. Clements call in a prescription for pain pills."

"These will be fine." I don't like taking medicine. So, Tylenol and Advil are about as heavy a drug as I'll consume. I swallow the pills. He helps me take a drink of water, my hands too shaky to hold the glass steady.

"Bath?" he asks when I know the man in him wants to take control and get it done.

"Please."

He encourages me to drink the rest of the water. I do. Then he sweeps me up and into the bathroom, setting me gently on the edge of the tub. "I'm going to undress you, Dani. Are you okay with that?"

This man has had his mouth, hands, fingers, cock on and inside my body. I'm surprised he's asking, considering I haven't rebuffed any of his kisses, but merely want more of whatever he's willing to give me. I appreciate him asking all the same. "Yes."

He gathers my hair, pulling it up. "I don't want to hurt you," he whispers as he kisses my cheek and gently secures my hair on top of my head with a large scrunchie. I don't want to know why he has one—

"It's yours. You left it here."

He kept it? "That was fortuitous."

He chuckles. "I suppose it was."

Have numerous women used it in the months since?

That thought is wiped from my brain as he starts to lift my shirt, slipping my arms out of each sleeve before pulling it over my head. "Okay?"

"Yes." He's so sure and gentle. His touch scorches my skin, reminding me of what I left behind that night, our connection so palpable, it's painful to fathom leaving him again when all I want to do is stay. "I'm sorry I'm not much help." Everything hurts; just sitting still, not jarring my ribs is difficult.

He captures my cheek. The sincerity in his eyes has mine pricking with tears. "Dani, you were in a train wreck. It's a miracle you and Henry didn't sustain grave injuries. You protected him with your body, held on to him so fiercely, I had to pry him loose. It's no wonder your limbs are weak. You're injured and worn out, baby."

29

His lips are so close. Close enough to… I tug him by his shirt, pressing my lips to his, wanting, needing the connection, reminding me I'm alive. Henry is alive. I didn't break my promise to Lucy.

His growl is feral when my tongue slips past his lips. I started the kiss. He quickly takes over, licking and tasting me like a treat. He's savory and sweet, and so powerfully male, I'd climb him if it wasn't for my ribs… and throbbing head.

"Dani." He pulls back. His panting breaths mix with mine. "Sorry—"

"Don't." He presses in for another heated kiss, sucking on my bottom lip before diving in for a quick sweep of his tongue. "You don't ever apologize for kissing me."

I wonder how he'd feel about sucking my breasts and touching me until I come undone. "Noted."

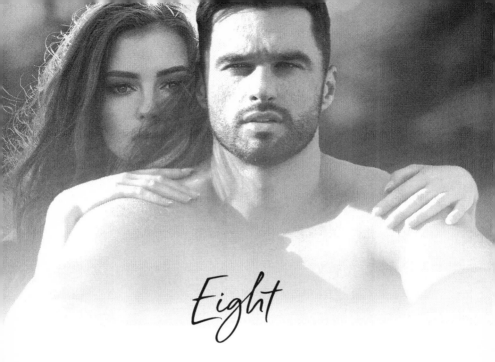

Eight

HER NIPPLES ARE HARD AS FUCK. SHE'S TURNED ON. I can smell her arousal as I pull her jeans and panties down her lovely legs that are now covered in bruises. *Baby*. My heart aches for what she's been through. My girl is hurting and so damn brave.

I kiss the largest of bruises on her left thigh, moving down and then up her right. She trembles, her grip on the edge of the tub tightening. I place her hands on my shoulders; she doesn't have the strength to hold on like that for long. She probably won't be able to move her fingers tomorrow as it is.

She sucks in air as I move up her side and kiss the purple bruising over her ribs. Tenderly, reverently, I make my way across her abdomen, up her arms to her neck.

I could have lost her today.

"Dani," I groan at the realization. I could have lost her and maybe have never even known it, never seen her again, and probably would have kept looking for her in every room until my dying breath. "Don't disappear on me. Promise."

She must sense my urgency as she squeezes me with a ferocity she shouldn't be able to manage and whimpers her reply, the emotions of the day getting to her too. I need to be strong for her. She's hurting and vulnerable and needs me to be careful for us both. I won't take advantage. "In you go."

Tugging my shirt over my head, I don't miss her eyes eating me up. My hungry redheaded temptress.

I cradle her in my arms and set her as gently as possible in the tub. I wait until she's settled before standing. Wiping my arms dry, I appraise her condition. *She's fine.* "I'm going to check on the soup. Don't drown."

Her biting her bottom lip as she eyes my cock pressing against my slacks tugs at my control. Tipping her chin, I garner her eyes. "Don't tempt me, my little runner. You're injured." Her blush is beautiful. "I'll be back."

Leaving the bathroom, I squeeze my cock, reminding it who's in control. I egotistically believe it's me, when I know good and well it's Dani who holds all the cards. Anything she needs, I'll gladly give her.

I take a few extra minutes dishing up soup for the both of us: hers, broth with a few veggies and shredded chicken; mine, more meat than soup to let my body cool down, my hormones taking a backseat to my logic.

She's hurt. *No sex.*

No sex.

No sex.

I continue my chant as I carry a tray of soup, dry toast, and water, setting it on the bathroom counter and nearly losing all control at the sight of her in my huge tub. It's swallowing her up; she needs company, arms wrapped around her.

No sex.

She needs my mouth on those tits.

That's not sex…

32

She needs my cock, pumping her through an orgasm or two. *No. Sex.*

I punch out a breath and hand her her mug of soup, watching to see if she can hold it steady. She does. I sit on the edge, palming my bowl, and eat as I watch her like a hawk.

There are no words beyond her *thank you* and my *welcome.*

She licks soup from the corner of her mouth. I swear I feel her tongue on my cock.

I grip my spoon to bring it to my mouth. She eyes it like I'm fisting myself.

She moans in appreciation. I groan in frustration.

Her eyes eat me up. Mine narrow as my control slips further and further away.

When we're done, I place our dishes on the tray, leaving them on the counter. I grab a washcloth and sink to my knees beside the tub, dipping my hand in to wet it. She smiles, closes her eyes, and tips her head back.

I'm going to hell.

I start at her face, washing small remnants of blood and dirt I missed earlier. Working my way down, she moans when I squeeze each breast, washing across her chest, straightening her shoulders to give me better access.

Straight to hell.

Before I make it past her stomach, her legs open, and water splashes my arm, her eyes begging me to touch her. "Dani," I warn."

She grips my wrist, guiding me lower. "Please."

"Fuck." I stand, pacing to the doorway and back, fisting my hair. "You're injured."

"Yes. Make me feel better." Her breathy voice nearly takes me to my knees.

"I don't want to hurt you further because I want you too much," I growl my confession.

33

"You won't." Her outstretched fingers barely reach mine as I stand beside the tub. "Please." It's that single word that packs a punch.

My chin hits my chest. "Slip forward," is all the warning she gets before I rip off my pants and underwear and slide in behind her, water splashing, my hard cock snaking down her back as I settle in and pull her onto my lap. The heat of the soapy water isn't nearly as hot as her naked and in my arms again. I fist the washcloth she hands me. "Lay your head on my shoulder and open your legs."

She does as I say, her smile pressed to my neck after a slight nip, her tits rising and falling with her deep breaths as she anticipates my touch.

"Don't gloat, baby." I slip my arms around her, one on her belly, holding her to me, and the other moving lower to wash her before I drag us both to hell.

Nine

GLOAT? I'M NOT GLOATING. I'M BEAMING WITH HAPPI-
ness and anticipation. "Flint," I gasp as he slips his skilled
hand between my legs.

"Try not to tense." He licks and sucks my earlobe just as the
cloth rubs across my clit, lower to my opening and lower still to
my— "Oh." I shudder.

"Shh, I got you. Breathe and relax." He washes as far as he
can reach down each leg and back, over my stomach and breasts,
and back between my legs.

Soon the washcloth disappears, and his hands touch with
the skill of a doctor who knows all my erogenous zones as if he
studied me for years in medical school.

"That's it, Dani." He squeezes my breast, twisting my nipple,
sending zings straight to my clit. He sucks my neck seconds before he slips a finger inside me. "Remind me how beautiful you
are when you come, my little runner."

I shiver at his choice of endearment. At the moment, I can't imagine running anywhere but into his arms, remaining just like this forever.

The water touches me everywhere, laps at my skin as he makes small waves with each movement. His fingers work magic, caressing and filling, making me ache in a whole new way, not from the wreck. I ache for more. I ache for him. It's physical yet not only. I ache for him in my soul, in my heart that has no room for another.

"Flint," I cry out, hurting, breaking for something I can't have. I can never...

He palms my mound, rubbing my clit, and slips more fingers inside, rubbing, fucking. It's not just physical, but— "Oh, God." Two strokes or a thousand, the buildup is immense. Too much. He grips me tighter, pressing my legs to the side of the tub with his, holding me steady, keeping me from moving, from grinding. I ask for more, and he gives and gives and gives until I...

"Fuck. That's it." He twists my nipples, keeping me coming. "Try not to thrash around, baby. Just absorb it." His breathing is rough, and his cock is rock hard below me. "Fuck. I've missed this body."

I arch, pressing into him, shaking, taking. His words inciting... "More," I moan. "Slip inside me," I plead.

"No." His stern response holds no argument. He's hard as stone, yet he doesn't plan on taking this further. Somehow the ache only grows. I want all of him.

"I need this. I need you. Remind me what it's like to be alive." Even if only for another night.

"Baby," he softens.

"Please, Flint."

"You'll be still. Not move a muscle," he commands. His tone sends goose bumps rippling across my skin.

"Yes." Yes, I'd promise anything just to feel him inside me

again, before it's too late, before reality comes crashing in, and I remember why I ran all those months ago.

You were scared.

I was. Our connection was intense. His soul-searching eyes zeroed in on me, and I was lost to his power, his draw, his hunger for me.

We couldn't get enough.

He couldn't get close enough.

He couldn't fuck me deep enough.

Then he did.

Only the more he gave, the more I needed—wanted.

I saw forever in his eyes, in his touch, in his words. And I ran, leaving the best part of myself behind.

Not a day has passed I haven't thought of him, looked for him in passing faces, loving Henry and Richard yet never feeling whole. What we lost. What I took from them. It's a daily reminder why running was the only recourse. But the wanting, the memories, the palpable viscosity of both have me hungry for more.

I whine when he removes his fingers.

He kisses my neck. "My impatient girl."

I preen from him calling me his. I want to be that. I want him to want that. Desperately.

The ache.

The ache.

The ache.

Slowly, painstakingly so, he pushes inside me, whispering dirty sweetness into my ear. Cursing, shaking, gripping me tight enough to hurt, yet it doesn't, he fills me. Deep, deep, deeper.

"My Dani," he exhales as if I satiate something in him sacred and cherished, as if I'm an answered prayer, a desired wish.

His tender touch sears my skin, heated traces of where he's been, marking, marking, marking me to my soul, leaving a trail, a pathway in and out—just for him.

Achingly slow, he moves, ripples in waves, undulating below me, gentle, loving, adoring. He takes me so completely; I am lost in his embrace. His hold, the only thing keeping me together, tethered to him in this moment, in this place, a watery cocoon of heat and lapping waves.

More, and more, and more he gives. Taking, taking, taking me higher, quenching my thirst, hydrating my soul. Filling, and filling, and filling.

With inciting words and molten touches, he liquifies me, sending me over the edge again and again before finally, finally filling me up, calling my name, answering my prayers with his pulsing release, his surrender to our connection.

For a moment, I am whole, complete, one—with him.

With him.

With him.

Ten

I AWAKE ALONE, THE SPACE BESIDE ME EMPTY. THE ROOM is still standing, not disheveled like it was the last time we came together—the last time she left me. My heart seizes, and my gut clenches, the emptiness of the room unbearable.

She's gone.

She promised.

She left me anyway.

I had her. In the palm of my hands, wedged into my heart, saddled next to my soul. I had her. She let me in. She ignited hope, fed the longing, filled the emptiness she left in my life eight months ago. And now…

Throwing off the covers, running down the hall with every intention of bolting out the front door to see if I can stop her, I come to a skidding halt across the room from my floor-to-ceiling view.

Arms crossed, head tilted, fully dressed, she studies me. "Good morning?"

She didn't leave.

She's still here.

She kept her promise.

"I thought you left." I sigh my relief, coming to a more natural stance. Though, my relief is short-lived as I assess, calculate what it'll take to breach the growing void between us. "You're still leaving—"

"You were coming to look for me like that?" she speaks over me.

"Yes."

Her brow shoots up at my response to her question. "Really?"

I shrug, ignoring my naked state, and move toward her. "I don't want you to leave. I would have chased you down in a blizzard—naked, if that's what it took."

"Well, I'm still here." She motions toward my bedroom. "You can dress. I'll wait."

The insatiable, begging-me-to-slip-inside-her version of Dani is gone. She's a fortress of resolve.

"I don't want you to leave," I try again in case she missed it the first time.

"I'm sorry. I have to." She steps around me, her needful eyes closed off, her desire hidden, tucked away. She's too good at that.

I can relate. I'm normally all business at the hospital—except where it came to her. But I don't want *the fortress of Dani*. I want my redheaded temptress who melts at my touch, surrenders to her desires. I want the woman who calls to me through time and space, who I want even more now than I did eight months ago. "Why?"

"I'll make coffee while you put something on."

"Dani."

My firm response has her softening. A small smile tips her

lips, and her eyes focus on me, the glimmer of aloofness falling away.

"Please, Flint." She kisses my cheek before her gaze drops and she moves to the kitchen.

"Don't leave," I demand before heading to my room to throw on track pants and a t-shirt before a bathroom pitstop.

When the scent of coffee fills the air, my nerves settle. She's still here, which means I have a chance of keeping her here, a chance at leaving an indelible mark on her soul, as she's left on mine. Remind her that what we've found—this connection, this heat—is not your standard, run-of-the-mill, one-night stand material. This *thing* between us is lock you down, make you mine, what love songs, movies, and books are about—a forever connection.

Coffee mug in hand, two sips down, I tug her to me. She comes willingly, sinking into my hold. I kiss her head and hold her tight. *Don't fucking leave me.* I sigh into her hair.

Never wanted this.

Never wanted *more*.

Now, I can't imagine never finding it.

Never wanting it.

Never finding *her*.

"I know you're scared, Dani. I appreciate you not running. But I'm not ready to give you up yet." I don't mention forever.

That'll have her sprinting *through* the door.

"I don't want to," she whispers into my chest, breaching my chest plate and wrapping around my heart.

I tip her chin, stealing her gaze. "Then don't." I kiss her warm lips and suck her coffee-flavored tongue till she whimpers, holding me like she never plans on letting me go. *Don't, baby. Never let me go.* "How about we start with breakfast?"

"Okay." She leans in, nuzzling into my neck, taking a deep breath before pulling back. "What can I do to help?"

I want to tell her to stay, for starters, but instead, "Sit, relax, drink your coffee, and tell me how you're feeling."

She wants to argue. This woman is not used to being pampered. I want to laugh. I'm not used to pampering women. We're in the same boat, out of our comfort zones, in uncharted territory—at least for me.

As she describes her current state of being, I check off the list in my head of all the areas of concern. "Tylenol every four hours or so, alternating with ibuprofen, will make your soreness manageable. No lifting anything heavy for a few weeks. No lifting Henry." I catch her frown over my shoulder as I sauté the onions, mushrooms, bell pepper, and sausage for the eggs. "A good rule of thumb is nothing heavier than a gallon of milk."

"Okay. I'll take it easy. But I can still help you. Can I break the eggs or something?"

"Sure." I kiss her head as she passes. "I want to check your staples after you eat."

"Sounds like fun."

I want to kiss her silly for opening up, lowering her walls, for the moment, at least.

We work well together, side by side, preparing breakfast. I have no doubt we'll be good at most things together.

"I was a nurse," she blurts after she finishes eating.

I put my fork down. She has my full attention.

"Well, I guess I still am." She frowns, staring at her empty plate. "But I'm not—"

"Working as one?"

Her pain-filled eyes meet mine. "No." Her soft reply is far more harrowing than that one word implies.

I palm her hand, wanting to pull her closer but settling for gentle contact. "What happened?"

"There was a shooting... many shootings."

Jesus. "Were you hurt?" I glance to her head, her fingers already there, moving along her scalp. There's a scar just to the left of the gash from the train wreck. In all the excitement of seeing her again, I forgot to ask about it.

"My sister and I were shot." She says it matter-of-factly, as if it's an everyday occurrence.

"Jesus." Before I can stop myself, I scoop her into my arms and sit as gently as possible on the long couch facing the windows. I've a million questions but remain silent, giving her time to share at her own pace.

"Some guy went on a rampage. Shooting up the hospital after losing his wife." Her tearful gaze locks on me. "My sister came every week, like clockwork, rain or shine. She never missed our Tuesday lunches, except when she gave birth to Henry, of course." The thought of Henry's birth has her smiling. "She was the best sister. She raised me after our parents died."

Henry's words come back to me: *My mom died when I was three.*

"Dani, I'm so sorry." I hug her tight, kiss her forehead, needing to imbue my sympathy over losing her sister and joy that my little runner survived.

She could have died, and I'd have never met her.

"It's my fault," my girl whispers.

"No." I capture her face, kissing her tears. "It's not." It can't possibly be.

"Henry and Richard lost Lucy because of me," she offers as if that's reason enough to hold this gut-eating guilt.

"No, they lost her because some guy chose to come to the hospital that day and take out his anger on innocent people. You couldn't have known or stopped him."

"She was protecting me."

Damn, I wish I had been there to protect her and her

43

sister. "It's a tragedy, Dani. You and your sister were victims. You didn't cause it."

She nods her consent, but her guilt is not that easily dissuaded. Does Richard know she blames herself? Does he blame her?

I hold her until her tears dry up, until she's calm and lax, until she asks me to take her home.

Eleven

THE RIDE HOME TO RICHARD'S IS QUIET BUT NOT THICK with regret or sorrow. I'm all cried out. My heart doesn't feel as heavy as it usually does when I think of Lucy and that fateful day twenty months ago.

It's *him*. He makes it better. The burden doesn't seem as insurmountable today.

"I didn't realize you lived with them." The roughness of Flint's voice shivers along my skin and throbs between my legs.

"I'm his nanny as well as his aunt." I open the car door to catch Henry as he flies into my arms before I'm barely unbuckled. I squeak from the impact but relish the warmth of his embrace and ignore the protest in my ribs.

"You're okay." He squeezes me tight. "I'm glad the hospital let you come home!"

I feel terrible I worried him but don't correct the assumption I was there overnight. I should have called. I wanted a night to myself—with Flint. I didn't want reality crashing down on me just yet, reminding me of my priorities, but lying to do it isn't right, or fair to Henry and Richard either. "I'm okay, little man. All good." I kiss his cheek and hold him, rubbing his back.

"Your aunt is sore, Henry. You need to be careful for a few weeks until she's healed." Flint holds the door open, encouraging Henry to ease up.

Henry climbs off my lap and faces Flint. "But she's okay, right, Dr. Heartgrove? You promised you'd takes care of her like she takes care of me."

Flint's serious gaze meets mine over Henry's shoulder as he kneels, getting eye level with my nephew. "I promise, Henry, I have every intention of taking good care of our girl, whether she wants me to or not." He raises his brow on the last piece.

I want him to, but...

"Doctors make house calls these days?" Richard calls from the front door.

"Only for the most important patients," Flint quickly replies. Gripping my hand, he helps me out of the car.

Henry runs to the house, but stops and turns. "Daddy and I are making grilled cheese. You want one, Dr. Heartgrove?"

"That depends." Flint secures me to his side, not missing my groan as my body protests all movement. "Are you making one for your aunt?"

Little hands propped on his hips, Henry gives us his biggest smile. "Of course, silly." He runs ahead, disappearing inside.

Richard steps back, holding the door open, his concerned gaze searching. "You're really alright?"

"Yes—"

"She will be with rest and no lifting," Flint steps on my response.

Richard glares at Flint instead of standing aside to let us pass. "Why are you here?"

"I'm taking care of the girl I lost eight months ago and have no intention of losing again." Flint shoulders past Richard, protecting me from hitting the doorframe. "Do you want to rest here or in your room?" He eyes the living space and up the stairs, frowning.

"My room is down the hall. Richard and Henry are upstairs."

That seems to satisfy him. I don't know if it's the stairs or the fact that I live with another man that's bothering him.

"Eight months ago?" Richard is as white as a sheet.

"Yes." No need to elaborate. It's not like I go out drinking often. It was one night. The anniversary of Lucy's death.

His gaze darts between me and Flint, working it out.

"I'll sit here until I get tired," I steer the conversation to safer ground.

"Daddy!" Henry calls from the kitchen. "It's burning."

"Shit!" Richard dashes for the kitchen, and I tense as I follow to fix our meal.

Flint stops me. "No. Sit. Relax. I'll see if I can help." Once I'm settled, he hovers over me. "I'm not letting you go, Dani. The sooner you come to terms with that, the easier this will all go."

"Who wants easy?" I try for nonchalance until I realize the double meaning. I did sleep with him the first night we met and last night.

He chuckles and kisses me soundly. "I'm not touching that one." He turns and heads to the kitchen. *Lord, help them. Lord help me.*

I sit back on the massive couch, put my feet on the ottoman, and close my eyes, listening to the sounds of two men and a boy making lunch.

Hours later, sequestered in Flint's arms on the couch, drifting in and out as he, Richard, or Henry chooses movie after movie, I notice Henry is asleep on Richard's chest as he naps in the recliner. The sight makes my heart ache.

"He's a good man." Flint's quiet baritone reverberates in his chest. "I'd like to go to his restaurant when you're feeling better."

My head lolls back so I can meet his gaze. "He seems to like you." Despite their rough meeting earlier.

"I'm glad. It will make it easier."

"What easier?"

"You and me."

Flint sighs when I just stare, dumbstruck. We're moving too fast for this to be real. But what if it is, or leads... No, it can't ever even get off the ground. I can't commit to him—to anyone—when my whole life revolves around the two asleep in the chair across the room.

Flint picks me up, carrying me to my room. "My little runner," he whispers in my hair, "not letting you go."

He sets me on my feet, helps me undress and ready for bed. Teeth brushed, medicine taken, he tucks me in with a kiss on my forehead. "Sleep tight." He taps my phone he set on the nightstand. "Call me if you need anything."

"G'night." I don't want him to leave, but it seems best, considering this isn't my house, and Henry likes to wake me up in the mornings. I'm not sure how he'd feel finding Flint in my bed.

He stops at the door, eyeing me over his shoulder. "I have rounds in the morning, but I'll call you. Promise you'll take it easy."

As if my ribs would let me do anything else. "Promise."

"I'll help you wash your hair tomorrow. It'll be easier on your ribs and laceration if you have help." His smile grows. "Not that I need an excuse to shower with you."

He leaves with a wink, and my blush only grows.

Apparently, I have a shower date.

That's a new one for me.

What does one wear to a shower date?

Nothing.

Twelve

ROUNDS CAME ENTIRELY TOO EARLY, ESPECIALLY considering my sleepless night. My little runner has been back in my life for barely two days, in my bed for only one of those, and I can't sleep without her. I wanted to charge over there at four this morning, an hour before my alarm went off, and climb in bed with her, hold her, close my eyes, and sleep for minutes, maybe seconds, but enough to feel like myself—the version that hasn't lost her.

Instead, I'm on my fifth cup of coffee after a fifteen-minute power nap, and on to my last patient to discuss their test results before I grab some lunch.

I knock before entering, hearing a gruff, "Come in," as I open the door and close it behind me.

Though pediatric neurology is my specialty, it doesn't mean I don't treat neuro patients of all ages. "Mrs. Giovanni." I smile at my patient and then her husband. "Mr. Giovanni."

"Doc, so glad you're here." Mr. Giovanni stands, holding his wife's hand. "It's the same questions. Over and over again."

"Antonio, why am I here? We're going to miss the wedding." Mrs. Giovanni glances at me and then quickly back to her husband, who patiently answers her questions she's no doubt asked a hundred times already.

"Mr. Giovanni—Mrs. Giovanni," I direct my conversation to the husband. Mrs. Giovanni won't remember any of this in 180 seconds. "All your wife's tests came back clean. No sign of stroke, brain bleed, or any other neurological issues."

"Then why can't she remember?" Mr. Giovanni's concern is evident and understandable.

"Your wife is suffering from Transient Global Amnesia. TGA for short. It's temporary and causes her to lose memories from, say, the last week or so, but most notably she can't form any new memories at the moment. She has no short-term memory, which is why she continues to ask the same questions every few minutes."

"What?! What does that mean? What caused it?"

"TGA is a temporary condition. An episode usually lasts twenty-four hours or less. Memories lost usually come back. But she will make no new memories until the episode passes, more than likely sometime overnight. By morning, your wife should be back to her pleasant self. Maybe a little confused because she won't know why she's in the hospital. I'd recommend getting a pad of paper and writing down her recurring questions and the answers. Then refer her to the pad each time the cycle begins again." I speak to Mrs. Giovanni, though, by the look on her face, she's totally lost. "I promise, this is a temporary situation; come tomorrow you'll be right as rain."

"What caused it? Will it happen again?" Mr. Giovanni settles in the chair, still holding his wife's hand.

They got married yesterday. The second for both of them. They were high school sweethearts who reunited six months ago. When he woke up this morning, he found his wife puttering around their honeymoon suite, confused, not remembering their wedding, and asking the same questions on repeat.

"The exact cause is not known. Migraines, high blood pressure, high cholesterol, changes in blood flow, low oxygenation, a shock in hot or cold water, head trauma, stress, some medical procedures, and sexual intercourse."

Mrs. Giovanni gasps. Mr. Giovanni frowns.

"I suspect, given your wedding and that we've ruled out all the other potential causes, it was a combination of stress and sexual intercourse that triggered the TGA."

"I fucked her into amnesia?" he deadpans, completely serious.

I try not to laugh, but holding it down to a smirk is the best I can do. "Potentially. It doesn't mean it will happen again. So don't worry about having sexual relations."

"Thank God," he sighs. "But it can happen again?"

"It can happen again. The statistics vary; on average, there's a nineteen percent chance of it recurring. The likelihood of it happening a third time is extremely rare." I continue to answer his questions and help him answer her questions when her memory resets and she forgets who I am or why she's here. I remind him to make a list of her questions with answers. It will make their day go much smoother.

"My associate Dr. Clements will be back to check on you tomorrow. The nurses are here for whatever you may need. But I anticipate you being able to leave tomorrow, say midafternoon."

"Doctor, why am I here?" Mrs. Giovanni asks with all the innocence of a woman who has no idea what's happening around her. She's remarkably calm.

I'm not sure I would be calm if I were in her shoes. I prefer to be in control, and not being able to remember anything, or remember that I can't remember, sounds like a nightmare. I spend a few more minutes with the couple, re-explaining to her as succinctly as possible. Then I slip out before the 180 seconds are up and the questions begin again.

Hot meal in hand, I scope out a secluded corner of the cafeteria to call my redheaded temptress.

Thirteen

MY RIBS PROTEST EVERY STEP AS I SHUFFLE TO THE kitchen seeking sustenance. I know being sorer the second day is normal, but, man, I didn't expect to feel this bad. Lack of sleep isn't helping. I couldn't get comfortable, missing my Flint pillow.

How can someone I spent two remarkable nights with, eight months apart, become essential to my wellbeing? I'd swear it was only hormonal if the loneliness in my soul and the ache in my heart weren't nagging me to believe it's *more*, something profound. I'm not sure I'm ready for *profound*, especially not this morning. Coffee may help. But damn, my ribs. I'm not sure I can reach the coffee cups.

I sigh in relief when I find Richard at the coffee pot. Thank God he's awake. "Could you pour me a cup too?"

"You're up." He seems relieved.

"Couldn't get comfortable."

He slides a mug of coffee my way and fills his travel mug.

"Going somewhere?" I thought he was staying home with Henry so I could rest.

"I was just getting ready to leave."

I glance at the clock. "It's six am. You were just going to leave me with Henry and not tell me?" So much for letting me rest today.

"I—" He waves at me. "You're up. You're fine, aren't you?"

I wouldn't say I'm fine, but he doesn't leave me room to answer.

His shoulders sag. "I missed work yesterday at the hospital and then watching Henry. I need to go in today."

He does usually work seven days a week. Taking the weekend off is not in his mindset, but his son and I were in an accident—surely his work won't mind. Shouldn't he want to stick around more than a day to be sure we're okay? At least Henry, if not me. "This early?"

"Deliveries." He sets the empty carafe in the sink.

Maybe he's too scared to contemplate what could have happened and is escaping into work... I sigh. I guess I'll be making more coffee if I have any hope of getting through today. No rest for the wicked.

"You got this?"

I pat his arm as I pass. "Go, but don't expect me to cook tonight."

His sigh of relief would've blown me over if I wasn't leaning against the sink. "I'll bring home dinner from the restaurant."

"Nothing greasy, please. I don't think my stomach can take it." Really, I'm just being catty. I'm tired. My perky is worn down—it got hit by a train yesterday.

I promised to take care of them, and I *want* to. But it'd be nice if he considered me in this equation, at least once. Or for him to recognize he's asking a lot of me in my condition. He's suffering. He misses Lucy. I'm sure seeing my face day in and day out is no consolation prize. He didn't plan on spending the rest of his life with me. He wanted the other redhead—the one he loved.

He mumbles his response and is out the door before I can even rinse out the pot to make more coffee. I take a deep breath. *I can do this.*

As the coffee percolates, I scramble some eggs. I'll keep a plate warm for Henry for when he wakes. He's five; stodgy eggs won't bother him, right?

I sip my coffee and pop a few slices of bread into the toaster. When it's all done, I steal Lucy's recliner for myself and eat my eggs and toast in the peaceful silence of the morning sun as it slowly rises over the house across the street.

Lucy loved mornings. She'd drink her coffee on the porch when Henry and Richard were still asleep and call me for a sisterly chat. It was our *thing*. Our time to bond, connect, before we started our day.

I miss you, Sis.

She's the first person I want to call with good news. The first person I want to reach out to when I've had a tough day. When the loneliness gets too... lonely. When Henry drives me crazy— love the boy, but still, he's a handful at times.

When I have a quiet morning, coffee in hand, my fingers twitch to call the only other person in this world who really cared if I existed or not. Okay, maybe a bit melodramatic. Henry cares. I know he does. But like Richard, his dependence on me is only because of the absence of my sister. If Lucy were still alive, she'd be the only one calling looking to be sure I was alright, not because she needed something from me, but because she cared and wanted to hear about my day, my successes, my challenges. She was always on my side, rooting for me.

I miss having someone unabashedly in my corner, on my side, pulling for me to succeed at life—whatever that would have turned out to look like. I doubt she ever thought it would be like this: me raising her son, being a pseudo wife to Richard in the most non-sexual way possible. She wanted more for me, a family. Turns out *this* is my more—hers.

When Henry wakes an hour later, my melancholy hasn't lifted, but he does shake the loneliness loose with his sleepy smile and cuddly hug. I get ten minutes of cuddles before he's bouncing on his feet, ready for breakfast of barely warm eggs and toast with avocado.

After breakfast, Henry plays quietly with his Legos and magnetic building set. I think he's going to be an architect, or a designer of some type. He loves to build, each new design more intricate than the last. I'm sure Richard hopes Henry takes over Rossi's Italian Bistro someday. I hope Henry discovers what *he* loves and finds a way to turn it into a living. Is a Lego Engineer a thing?

My phone rings while I'm working on lunch. My excitement when I see Flint's name on my screen is unsettling.

Maybe he cares if I exist or not.

Don't get ahead of yourself. You can't keep him.

When I hear his deep rumble on the other line, it's hard to remember why. "How's my little runner?"

Fourteen

"I'M GOOD." THE LIE STICKS IN MY THROAT, MAKING ME sound more desperate than I'd ever want him to know. "You sure? Would you tell me if you weren't?"

His intuitiveness is unnerving. "Probably not."

His unbridled chuckle turns to a growl. "I wish you would." He has no idea what he's asking for. He'd never want the burden of all I carry inside. My emotional brain dump on him would surely scare him off. He'd be *my* little runner then.

"Are you resting? Letting Richard take care of you?"

The reminder of this morning has my vision prickling. "Um—"

"Dani, you need to rest as much as you can. Don't overdo it. Think if you got dizzy and passed out. You could hit your head. Get another concussion or worse."

I didn't consider that. "I'm a nurse," I blurt as if that's explanation enough or why I'm suddenly light-headed. I sit at the kitchen table, breathing deeply and slowly. But when it's not enough, I lie on the kitchen floor and close my eyes.

"Dani?"

"Aunt Dee?" Henry comes running. "You 'kay? You don't looks so good." He takes the phone from my ear. I'm too weak to protest. "Who's this?"

"Henry?" I can hear Flint's concern. "Where's—"

"You said you'd takes care of her! She's laying on the floor—"

I roll over and manage to crawl to the trashcan before I lose what's left of my breakfast.

"She's throwing—"

The sound of my puking overrides whatever else Henry says to Flint.

"—white like a marshmallow."

Little hands pat my back. "It's okay, Aunt Dee. Flint and me are gonna takes care of you." He hands me a kitchen towel, then disappears into the living room, chatting away on the phone but pausing to listen to whatever Flint is saying in return.

"Okay. I gots it." He places my phone on the counter.

"Dani, I'm on my way," Flint's voice comes alive in the kitchen. I glance at Henry.

"Dr. Heartgrove asked me to puts him on speaker. He's worried. I'm worried." My little man touches my shoulder.

"I'll be fine, Henry. Don't worry." I give him the best smile I can manage. I should have seen this coming. The way I felt when I woke up, worse than I did yesterday. I'm a nurse, for God's sake. I'm acting like the worst patient ever, ignoring doctor's orders just to not rock the boat with Richard. He should have stayed home. I should have insisted. I close my eyes and breathe in through my mouth and out my nose. I can't upset Henry.

"—take me longer than I'd like. I'm sending someone over to help you and Henry until I get there. Henry, do you have the pillow?"

"Yes, I gots it.""

"Good, help your aunt lie down where she is. If she needs water, can you get her some?"

"Yes. She's already gots a cup. I'll get it." Henry runs out of the room.

"Dani—"

"You don't need to come. I'm feeling better already." I settle on my side after stretching to turn off the stove.

"Can Henry open the door when my friend gets there?"

"You don't—"

"Dani, you need help. Henry is being brave, but he's scared. His favorite person is lying on the floor in the kitchen."

How can I argue with that? I never want to scare Henry. He's lost enough. "Okay." I swipe at my eyes. I can't scare Henry like this.

"I'll be there as soon as I can."

"Thank you."

"You can thank me by staying there until help arrives."

"My knight in—"

"I'm no knight, Dani. I'm tempted to show you how un-knightly I am—"

"Little ears," I remind him.

"Henry?"

"Yes, sir?"

"You take care of our girl until my friend gets there, okay?"

"Emily."

"That's right. Her name is Emily. She's going to knock on the door, say yours and Dani's names, and give her name. Then you can let her in. If something happens, and you get scared, you call 9-1-1. You got that, Henry?"

Henry puffs out his chest. "I gots it, Dr. Heartgrove."

"Good. I think you can call me Flint now, Henry."

"Okay, Dr. Flint."

His chuckle is comforting. "Be brave, Henry. It's only a little longer before Emily gets there."

"Imma take care of Aunt Dee."

"That's my boy. Dani?"

"Yes?"

"No heroics. Stay where you are. If you don't—"

"No threats. I understand."

His deep sigh echoes along my skin. "I only make promises I intend to keep, my little runner." The gruffness in his voice has me closing my eyes. I'm thankful he's coming, but I regret the reason.

Richard shouldn't have left me with Henry.

I should have stood up for myself and insisted he stay or take Henry with him. Not that a professional kitchen is any place for a child, but Richard practically grew up there—it's his family's restaurant, after all. The least he could have done was dropped him off somewhere safe.

When Flint hangs up, Henry grabs another pillow and lies on the floor facing me, holding my hand. "Why's Dr. Flint call you *little runner*?"

My heart skips, and a smile tugs at my lips. Should've known he'd latch onto that. "Sometimes, Henry, the way a person makes you feel can be scary. I don't mean like *they're* scary. But how much you like them and want to be with them all the time can be scary, especially if you don't have much room for that person in your life." *And you're scared of losing them.* I'm not sure I could stand to lose another person.

His little brow furrows in concentration. "Like how much Daddy loves Mommy?"

I run my hand over his strawberry-blond bangs. "Yeah, kinda like that."

"And it scares you so's you runs away?"

"Yeah, I kinda ran away after meeting Dr. Heartgrove for the first time."

"Because you loves him?"

"Maybe?" This little man, dragging it all out of me. He doesn't have a clue he's asking things that are too soon in a relationship to be asking. And here I am telling him like he's an adult and not a five-year-old boy. He'll forget all of this, right? "I'm not sure it's love. But I really like him."

"He loves you." He says it without doubt, no question. Such innocence and trust. I hate to see him lose that someday.

We're saved by a knock on the door. "Henry? I'm Emily. Dr. Heartgrove sent me over to check on you and Dani. Can you let me in?"

Henry jumps to his feet but hesitates, looking at me.

"It's okay. You can let her in."

He bolts for the door, unlocks and swings it open. "Hi. I'm Henry."

"Hello, Henry." I can barely make out a dark-haired woman bending to stick out her hand. "It's nice to meet you." She stands and spies me over Henry's head. "Hi, Dani. I'm Mrs. Heartgrove."

Mrs. Heartgrove? Shock has me believing this kind, beautiful woman is Flint's wife. He's married, just my luck.

You can't keep him.

Obviously not. He's married... to a stunning older woman.

Oh my God! I'm a cheater.

No. He's the cheater. I'm the other woman.

She brushes her dark hair over her shoulder; eyes rimmed in dark lashes take in my sorry state. Some impression I'm making.

I'm banging her husband! Oh my god. I'm going to hell.

She smiles, concern and humor dancing in her eyes. "I'm Flint's momma."

Fifteen

NOT HAVING A LIFE HAS ITS PERKS WHEN I'M ABLE to call on fellow doctors to cover my patients. I've worked extra holidays, vacation coverage, and grunt shifts for years. I didn't mind volunteering to take the awful shifts. Again, I had no life. I happily worked so they could spend time with their families. But not today. Today is my turn to call in IOUs and get the next couple of days covered so I can take care of Dani as I know she needs to be taken care of. I never should have left it to Richard. He's a nice guy, but he's used to taking advantage of Dani's kindness, exploiting her guilt over her sister's death to his advantage.

And if he didn't understand the seriousness of the situation before, I'll correct that so Dani's never put through the stress of what happened again.

I let myself in, noting Richard's car is missing from the driveway. He and I need to have a talk but not before I check in on my girl and Henry.

I find my mom in the kitchen stirring a pot on the stove

and Henry drawing at the kitchen table, his tongue sticking out to the side as he tries to make a circle. He does a pretty good job.

"Hey, Henry." I muss his hair before striding to my mom to give her a kiss on the cheek. "Thanks, Mom."

"Hi, Dr. Flint," Henry distractedly replies, focusing on his masterpiece.

"No thanks needed." Mom pats my cheek.

I take in the familiar aroma of Mom's cooking. "Spaghetti?"

"Yep." She nods to Henry. "He's a sweetheart, said spaghetti was one of his favorites."

"It's my absolute favorite," Henry confirms, eyes still on his paper.

"That's good." I take the seat next to him. "You doing okay, Henry?"

He sets down his pencil and folds his hands over his paper. "I'm okay. How are you?"

This kid. He's entirely too mature for his age. "I was really worried earlier, but I'm better now that I'm here."

"Were you scared?" he asks in a whisper that's hardly a whisper at all.

I lean in, whispering back, "I was. Thank you for taking care of our girl. You were brave."

He beams, leaning in, placing his hand on my shoulder. "Aunt Dee is feeling better. Emily tolds me she's resting, and I should be quiet. I'm being so, so quiet."

"That's good, Henry."

His smile falls. "Dr. Flint?"

"Yeah?"

"She's scared."

Concern has my heart thumping harder. "Scared," I confirm.

"Yep. She's scared of you."

Shit. Was I too rough on the phone? Too demanding? Or did she say something about the night before? "Of me?"

He frowns. "No, that's not right." He scratches his nose and tries again. "She's not scared *of* you. She's scared of her feelings *for* you. You know, 'cause she runs."

My little runner.

"Are you sure you're only five?" my mom asks over my shoulder, placing a bowl of spaghetti in front of Henry, careful to remove his papers first.

"I'm sure. I'll be six in…" he silently counts on his fingers, "in three months."

Five going on thirty-five. "I appreciate you sharing that with me, Henry." I suspected, but the question is, why does *he* know this little detail? What in the world happened here today? Henry said she was scared, but confessing emotions is next-level scared for Dani.

Mom encourages me to check on Dani, *after* I call Richard, so he knows what he's walking into. I don't really care to give him a heads up, but I'd rather do it now and stay with Dani than have to come out and deal with him when he gets home to a house full of people.

My first call goes unanswered. He's probably like most people; if the number is unrecognized, you send it to voice-mail. I text him to let him know it's me. When my text shows as *read*, I call again.

"Hey, everything okay?" He sounds out of breath.

"Not really, no. You were supposed to stay home and take care of Henry so Dani could rest for the next few days."

He clears his throat. "I had to work."

The announcement of, "Gentlemen, give a warm welcome to the lovely Twilight on the center stage," sidetracks my thoughts. What the ever-loving fuck?

"I didn't realize you work at a strip club." He's not at his restaurant as he's led Dani to believe. He's at a fucking titty bar having a good time while she's here suffering, watching *his* kid.

"Rossi's is not a strip club." A door shuts, and the club music dies away. "But I am working."

"Really?" There's a story here. I can't force him to confide in me. But I can't stand by and not try to make this right for Dani—for Henry. "Listen, I don't really need context around what you're doing. I only care that you left Dani with Henry when she's in no condition to take care of herself, much less him. When I left last night, you were staying home to watch Henry. You agreed."

"What happened?" Finally, he sounds like the concerned father and brother-in-law I met only yesterday.

"Dani nearly fainted while making lunch. She got sick in the kitchen. Luckily, I called right before it happened, and Henry was able to talk to me and fill me in on what was happening."

"Fuck."

"Yeah, I left the hospital as soon as I could, but I sent my mom over in the meantime. I just got here. Henry is eating spaghetti. My mom will stay and watch him until you get home. I'm going to check on Dani and take care of her."

"God, Flint. I'm so sorry. I really thought—"

"Save your 'sorry' for Dani. You put your needs over hers, or Henry's. That's not acceptable. My mom will come back every day to take care of Henry while Dani recovers. I'll be here too. Dani is my priority."

"I need to be at work; I don't know how—"

"We've got you this week, Richard. But next week, if Dani's still not up to it, you need to make other arrangements. I'm supporting her, not stepping in for you."

"Yes. Yes, of course." He's quiet for a moment, then, "Henry and I are moving."

"What?!" My insides drop. I just found her again, and I'm losing her already? She nearly died two days ago. It means something that she came into my ER, back into my life. I can't let her go, not without taking a chance on us.

"I need to be closer to work. That house, that town was Lucy's dream. She wanted to be closer to Dani. I was willing to deal with the commute before, but with Henry starting kindergarten in the fall, it makes sense to move now."

I didn't see this coming. "What about Dani? Are you expecting her to just uproot her life and move with you? Or are you abandoning her when you're her only family?"

"We haven't talk specifics. I'd hoped she'd come with us, keep watching Henry. He loves her, and she doesn't have a life—"

"Because she's living for you and Henry. She loves you both, but it's her guilt that keeps her here. She gave up her job for you both. Now you expect her to move away too?"

"I don't expect—"

"One week, Richard. You have one week to figure out your shit. But know this: I have no intention of losing Dani again. If she really wants to move, that's her choice, but don't use your dead wife to guilt her into making your life easier by continuing to give up hers."

I disconnect.

On a sigh, I return to the kitchen and give Mom a quick update on Richard and the plan for the week, working hard to keep my anger in check. With Mom on board, I kiss Henry's head, wishing him goodnight.

"Takes care of our girl, Dr. Flint." Henry stops me in my tracks.

"I've got her, Henry," I assure him.

"Don't lets her run." He stabs me in the heart with that little encouragement.

"Don't plan on it, little man." I look at Mom, her eyes misty. She wants grandkids. She wants *this* for me. "You be good for Emily. Your dad will be home later."

"I will. I promise." His last words hit hard. He's only five, and yet he knows the importance of promises kept and those broken.

I don't intend on breaking any promises to him or my little runner.

Sixteen

SOMETHING STIRS ME. OPENING MY EYES, I FIND THE light brown ones I've dreamt about for so many months hovering over me. Is he really here? "Am I dreaming?"

The quirk of his lips precedes the gentle touch on my cheek. "I think I'm the one who's dreaming, to have found you again."

"Sweet talker." I pull him down for a kiss, thankful I took the time to brush my teeth before lying down.

It's a soft, chaste kiss, only the press of his mouth to mine, for a count of one-two-three, yet it confirms I'm not dreaming. He can stir my banged-up body into believing sex is in my near future, even when I see the denial and self-restraint in his eyes.

"How are you feeling? The truth," he insists.

I've no intention of lying, but maybe not divulging the entire truth. "Sore, stiff, tired, but better now that you're here."

He studies me for a moment before nodding, kissing my cheek and standing. "Do you need anything?" He slips off his shoes and socks.

"Besides you?"

He stops unbuttoning his shirt, his heated gaze flashing to mine. "My redheaded temptress, you have me."

My tummy flutters with butterflies, and a shudder ripples along my skin. Do I? "I'm such a mess."

"*My* beautiful mess." He continues to strip until he's only in his boxer briefs, his clothes slung over my reading chair in the corner.

He moves like a panther, every sinewy muscle flexing below his skin. He starts at the end of the bed, traveling up my body on all fours. On instinct, I want to back away, but fight it. He's powerful, daunting, and focused all on me, and I'm a disaster on two legs on a good day.

He lowers until he's hovering, nose to nose. "I see you, my little runner. I see the fear in your eyes. The uncertainty of us, of your place in the world." He presses a kiss to my forehead, each cheek, and finally my lips. I sigh into his touch, tension leaving my body as he gently settles over me, holding his weight but ensuring I feel him everywhere. "I've got you, Dani."

His tenderness has my eyes pricking with unshed tears. Closing them, I pull him in for a deeper kiss, breaching his lips before he can delve into mine. He tastes like home and happily ever after.

He growls in approval, or perhaps disapproval, when I open my legs to feel him more intimately.

It's not enough. In frustration, I rip at the covers between us.

"Hey." He grips my hand, bringing it to his lips. "You're going to hurt yourself." His mouth consumes mine before I can protest, believing he's going to put a stop to this.

I moan into his mouth when he skillfully removes the covers, resumes his position between my parted legs, and slowly grinds his hips.

I say a silent prayer to all things holy.

This man. He does me in.

Rocking with him, warmth traveling to my core, need surging, I urge him forward.

Our heated kiss turns hungry, passion-filled, lusty, and yet more loving than any touch I've ever felt. It's him. It's always been him. In the months since our first encounter, it was him I craved, fantasized of, dreamt about.

Searching, I grip his ass under his briefs. Wanting them off, I tug and tug. He breaks our kiss, a rough "Baby" breathed between us.

"Need you, my knight."

He devours my mouth to protest me calling him my knight. He may hate it, but I love it. It fits. He's a modern-day knight in shining armor, saving lives, and wreaking havoc on women's libidos as he moves through the world.

I manage to push his underwear down his thighs, his impressive hard-on popping free and teasing me in the most devilish of ways.

"Dani," his sterner protest only makes me hotter.

"Need you," I remind him, as if he could take my actions for anything else but a woman who needs to be loved by her man.

My man.

Damn, love the sound of that. I don't know how or if I can make that work, but at the moment, it seems to be working just fine.

"Slow," he concedes, the twinkle in his eyes eating me up as I pull my shirt up, only to have my hands stilled and him take over the task of getting me naked.

A sharp stab in my ribs has me acquiescing. Besides, his hands on me and his heated gaze are enough to send me to the twelve realms of heaven.

I come off the bed when he latches onto my nipple. With a growl, he weighs me down, holding me still with his body, making me take every delicious morsel of pleasure.

When he traverses lower, wet, heated kisses leaving a trail of goosebumps, my nipples tighten painfully. I stop his progress, seeing the intent in his eyes. "There's no time for that."

His brows rise. "There's always time for eating my girl." He rubs his nose along my seam, then stares at my cropped hair. "My redheaded temptress."

I blush at his appraisal. I thought he called me that because of the hair on my head, but maybe it has a more lascivious meaning. I clench around nothing... "Need you inside." His eyes dart to mine. "Fill me."

His growl is no deterrent.

"Why do you make me beg?"

His smile is immediate. "I love you needy for me, my little runner."

"I'm so needy it hurts." I tug on his arms.

He slowly trails kisses up my stomach, over each breast before teasing both with his hands and mouth. "I've craved you every second of every day since we met, Dani." He nips at my peak before sucking deeply, only to release it with a pop.

Settling higher, he widens my legs with his. "Slow," he practically growls when he presses forward, penetrating, gliding through my slickness, pulling a gasp from my lips only to be consumed by his. "So fucking mine," he teases across my lips. "Say it."

Damn, love him possessive, taking what I'm so easily offering. "You're mine," I tease.

"Damn straight." He pulls out, holding. "Say it." It sounds like a command, but the vulnerability in his eyes speaks volumes. He *needs* me to say it, believe it.

I cup his cheek, locking eyes. "I'm yours." *Only yours, even when I'm not—I'll still always be yours.*

He thrusts hard enough to take my breath, claiming, marking, taking me with every drive of his cock, flick of his tongue, and dirty words of praise.

Filling my body.

Filling my soul.

Filling my heart.

He banishes the darkness, dulls the guilt, feeds the longing.

I wrap around him, pulling, clenching, sucking his body with my hands, mouth, pussy, and legs, taking him into myself in every possible way. I devour his passion, his pleasure, feasting on his moans, sighs, pants, and possessive growls.

Rising higher and higher, my breath a casualty of our joining, I fight to keep up. Fight to stay in control. Fight to watch him come apart above me, inside me, for me.

"Dani, baby," he whispers to my soul, grabbing my ass, changing the angle of his thrusts.

My legs shake as tingles ignite and flash through my limbs to my core, tightening my nipples, forcing my head back. Ecstasy escapes my lips as I'm thrown over the edge. Blinding light. Ringing ears. Joining. Pounding. Pounding. Pounding. I come so hard, I lose sight, exploding around him, sucking him deeper, clenching and begging.

"Jesus Christ," he barks seconds before he fills me, giving me what I seek: his ultimate pleasure, his surrender, his love if only for the moment. I am everything to him in this very second, having rocked his world as much as he has mine.

Becoming one is no joke. It's the ultimate gift. The tie that binds. The revelation and proof of life.

He. Is. Life.

And in this moment, he is mine.

Seventeen

I think I've died. The waning tremors of my release shoot the last of my cum against her cervix. She shudders and squeezes my cock as if she can feel it.

Pregnant. The thought echoes in the back of my brain.

Jesus. We didn't use a condom. Didn't the last time either. The realization has me stilling, waiting for the familiar panic at the idea of commitment to set in. It doesn't come.

I want to get her pregnant.

The idea settles and stirs my cock. She trembles and sighs.

I love you is all I can think when her sex-wrung gaze meets mine.

Jesus Christ.

I kiss her nose, slip out and off her, and stumble to the bathroom. It's the endorphins and oxytocin. I'm sex-high. My reflection in the mirror doesn't convince me that what I'm feeling isn't real.

Love. Pregnant.

Never thought I'd fall down that rabbit hole.

Well, I did when I met my redheaded temptress eight months ago. I knew then she could bring me to heel. But she's not even trying. I don't think she even wants to keep me. And I've fallen anyway.

Fuck. Me.

I eye my cock, think twice before washing her off me, then rewet the washcloth with hot water to take care of her.

She's sitting on the edge of the bed, sheet pulled across her body. Her head hangs low, studying a spot on the floor.

God, did I do that? Did I hurt her? Does she feel used?

She's injured, asshole.

Twice I said I wasn't going to have sex with her, and twice she's broken my resolve, putting her injuries on the back burner to feed our hunger.

I kneel at her feet, brushing her hair from her eyes. "Dani?" A tear drops to her lap, then another, and another. "What's wrong?"

She shakes her head. Her eyes plead. Her mouth remains silent.

"Did I hurt you?"

Her eyes widen. "No," she whispers, falling back on the bed like a woman without hope.

What the hell happened between me slipping out of bed and coming back to clean her up?

I had a major revelation. Did she have one too? By the looks of it, she's not happy with whatever's going on in her head.

"Dani, talk to me. I can't help if I don't know what's going on." I hover over her, kiss her temple, down her cheek, nudging her to look at me.

When our eyes meet, her lips part, close, then open again. "I can't."

The anguish in voice tugs at my insides. "Can't what?"

"Whatever you're thinking. I can't." More tears.

The fact she's crying reveals she cares. Does she love me? Does she see a future with me even if she's scared? "We can figure it out."

"He's moving."

Fuck. Richard. I glance to the nightstand, where her phone screen is still lit up. He must have texted her, and she's decided to go with them. Is this her way of breaking up before giving me a chance?

"Richard and Henry are moving. He just told me. He's been toying with the idea, but I didn't really know plans were already in motion."

I shake my head. "You don't have to go. Stay here with me." Yeah, I'm *that* asshole asking her to choose me over the only family she has left.

"I can't. I promised." The pain in her voice is mirrored on her face.

Can't she see she's ripping out my heart?

I can't fight the memory or the promise made to a dead sister. Who can compete? "I don't think your sister expects you to give up your life to be a substitute for her. Would she want you to abandon any dreams of your own? Do you plan on marrying Richard? Becoming his wife?" The thought of that stabs at my soul that's screaming, *she's mine.*

"No!" She shoots from the bed, grabbing her silk robe off the hook in the bathroom. "It's not like that. You know it isn't." She pulls the sash tight, her hips and boobs highlighted by the thin lavender fabric.

I can't lose her, and she's misunderstanding. "I'm not saying me or them. We can make it work. I could open a practice there—*we* could open a practice." Damn. I haven't considered private practice in a long time. It'd be better hours, especially

75

if I found a partner or two, and with her as my nurse—it's perfect.

More tears fall. "I wish—"

"You don't have to wish, Dani. I'm right here. Offering you... everything." *Anything. Please, fuck. Say yes.*

"I want to."

I hug her to my chest, gripping her back and sinking my fingers into her hair. "Think about it. We can make it work. Give *us* a chance." I tip her chin till we're nose to nose. "Fight for me, Dani. Fight for us."

"Flint." The way she begs—for me—is my undoing.

There are no more words.

The need in her eyes, the hunger of her touch is all I need to take her, consume her, lose myself *in* her.

It's fast, passion-fueled, ignited by fear, loss and hope.

Pinned to the wall, she chants, "Harder."

I surge forward, devouring her mouth as she claws my back in an effort to draw me into her one molecule at a time. "I could live right here for eternity."

"Fuck," she gasps.

Her dirty, sexy mouth punctuates her grip on my cock. It's too fucking good. So perfect, I'm light-headed. I lock my knees and press into her, keeping my feet under us. A beat or two until I'm steady enough to drill her into the wall, echoing her cries with grunts.

She's ravenous, fucking me back like it's the last time we'll be together. Like I'm the last cock she'll ever let inside her.

Damn. My rhythm slips. Is that what this is? A goodbye fuck? "Dani?"

Unfettered tears stream down her cheeks. "Don't stop."

"Never." *Never stopping—if this is the only way I can have you, I'll nail you to this wall without end.*

"Fuck, baby." I spill inside her as she cries out my name

when her orgasm hits. I slam into her harder than her injured body deserves, but her quakes of pleasure spur me on until the very last drop is spent and drips between us.

I love you is on the tip of my tongue.

Jesus. I do, don't I?

I bury my head in her neck, trying to catch my breath and my bearings.

She mumbles into my hair. Her grip on me tightens, not letting me slip from her heated walls.

Home.

She's become my home.

"I can't," her murmur finally hits its target.

I fight her grip, trying to keep my girl close while her words push me away. "Don't," I plead.

"I can't," she cries, crumpling to the floor.

Fuck. Fuck. Fuck. I grip my hair. My world collapses around us—me.

My little runner. Fuck. Me. Fuck my heart.

Unable to leave her on the floor, I pick her up, placing her on the bed, holding her face between my hands, swiping at her tears. "I can." I kiss her red, puffy lips, take in her disheveled, sexy state and step back.

Turning away, I collect my clothes, ignoring her sobs behind me.

She can't choose me. Her guilt won't allow it.

"I can't," she cries as if I didn't hear her the multiple times she said it before.

"I know." I pull on my clothes as fast as possible. Then I turn, memorizing my little redheaded runner. *I love you.* I clench my jaw, locking in those words not fit for her.

"I can't," she whispers.

I eat up the space between us and kiss her. One. Last. Time. "Fight for us," is the last thing I say before I leave.

They aren't the three words I want to leave her with, but perhaps they are more important in this moment.

Choose me, my soul screams as I stomp away, shards of my shattered heart trailing behind.

Eighteen

I MANAGE TO DRAG MYSELF OUT OF BED HOURS LATER, MY body in dire need of water and food. I should starve to death. It would serve me right for the way I treated Flint. He'd never treat me in kind.

As I nibble on a banana, Richard traipses in, beer in hand, defeat all over his face. "I'm sorry."

A heartless chuckle escapes before I rein it in. "What are you sorry for?"

"Flint. I saw him leave. He was upset. I'm sorry. I should have waited to tell you about moving. It was piss-poor timing."

That's the truth. "Poor timing seems to be our motto," I mumble into my glass of milk, downing it in one long swallow.

Why couldn't I have met Flint before Lucy died, when my heart was open and available for the taking? Though it seems destiny is on my side, bringing him into my life again, nothing has changed. My future—my focus—is still on Henry. How could it not be? The reason I left Flint in his disheveled, well-used bed eight months ago is the same.

Destiny is just being a cruel bitch, rubbing him in my face, along my heated body, inside my lonely soul.

Lost for words, Richard stares out the kitchen window into the backyard that used to be his haven. He loved to barbeque, even if it was just the three of them. I came over whenever I could, but I was never around much. This was their sanctuary. I didn't like to intrude. Richard always worked so hard, affording Lucy the luxury of staying home with Henry, and they always sounded so happy.

I never had a clear picture of my future. I vaguely had the idea of a husband and kids, but I didn't see it as brightly as Lucy did. A part of me was afraid if I sought happiness, it would strike me down like it did our parents.

Flint calls me an optimist. I don't see it. I don't see a way around this obstacle. But God knows I yearn for a future with Flint now. Now that I can't have it, I see it so clearly—or at least a piece of it. The man I'd want at my side as my partner.

I think me stepping into Lucy's life was so easy because I didn't have a clear sense of my own, beyond a job I wasn't all that crazy about. It wasn't my passion, or maybe I was too blind to see what I had. To be thankful for what I had: a great job, great friends, a sister who loved me, watched out for me, and Henry. My sweet Henry. He deserves brothers and sisters, and cousins.

I could give him cousins.

"She was pregnant," Richard's grated admission studders my thoughts.

"Oh my God." I grip the counter.

"She was planning on telling you that day."

Oh, dear God. I bend over, the room spinning, my pulse hammering in my ears.

Breathe. I can't breathe.

Strong hands guide me to a kitchen chair. "Fuck. Breathe, Dani."

I'm trying.

She was pregnant.

I'm going to hell.

She said she had something to tell me, but we never got to it because some asshole shot up my hospital, killing her.

She was pregnant.

Killed her unborn baby.

Straight to hell.

No, I'm in hell.

"Dani—"

"Please, stop." I struggle but manage to escape, relishing the sting in my ribs and the throb in my head. I deserve it. It should have been me.

Why wasn't it me, God?

Why wasn't it me?

When morning comes, I feel worse than I did the day before. If it wasn't for my broken heart and body, I'd wonder how that's even possible.

Clanging in the kitchen has me moving at a speed that shouldn't be possible, given my state. I freeze in the doorway when Emily comes into view at the stove where I left her yesterday.

"Emily?"

Her kind smile lands on me but quickly fades. "Oh, my, Dani." She hurries over. "You look like you're about to fall over. Come take a load off." She ushers me into a chair with little protest.

"Why are you here?"

"My son sent me to assist you until you're better." She stands, hands on her hips, with me locked in her gaze. "If you could see what I see, you'd know why I was here."

"But Flint and I—"

"Hush now. You and Flint having a tiff is no reason for me to back out on my commitments. I promised to help out through the end of the week, and I intend to do just that." She pats my hand, giving me a look that says she'd stay longer if I needed her to.

"You're a saint." I had no idea how I was going to make it through taking care of Henry today. He'd have done his best to be quiet and easy, but he's five. He deserves better than what I'm able to give him at the moment.

Her laugh is joyful. Everything about Emily Heartgrove is joyful and light. Her son may be a little domineering at times, but the resemblance in looks and temperament are recognizable.

He tried to bring you light, but you refused him.

"Dani, I'm far from a saint. But I do love children, and since my sons refuse to give me grandbabies of my own, I make do with little angels that come into my life." She's genuinely happy to be here helping.

Thank you, Flint. "Thank you. I can never repay you."

She stops and turns, her brow raised. "Actually, you can."

Uh oh. "How?"

She taps her lips for a second before a devilish smile breaks free. "I'll tell you at the end of the week."

"I'm a little afraid of you, Emily Heartgrove." I stand, making my way to the coffee pot. "But I'm too desperate to kick a gift to the curb."

She sets the cream next to my cup. "You should be afraid. I'm a momma bear where it comes to my sons."

I stir in sugar and creamer, unable to look her in the eye for fear she'll see the regret and heartbreak swimming there in unshed tears. I blink, looking away, swiping as they fall. "He's lucky to have you."

Whatever she has planned for me hurting her son, I deserve. I'll take it like a big girl. Adulting sucks. No one knows that better than me.

As the week progresses, I'm able to do more and begin to feel more like my old self, physically at least.

My heart, I've given up any hope of fixing. It's broken, and only one man can repair it. But that's impossible when I'm a moving target. Literally.

We move in two weeks. Richard never outright asked me to come, but he didn't say he didn't want me to move with them. He made sure there was a room for me, should I want it, like it's a given.

It's like an unspoken rule: we don't talk about moving on from Lucy. At first, I thought me helping out was moving on, moving forward, but I'm beginning to see that I'm only a crutch, helping us both hobble along, moving but covering little ground.

By Friday, I join Emily and Henry on their walk to the park. There's a little spring to my step, and the morning sun feels good on my light skin that's a package deal with red hair.

Emily hands me a little tub of sunscreen. "Be careful you don't burn. My son would never forgive me."

I squeeze some on my hand and give it back to her. "No offense, Emily, but I doubt he'd care. Not with how things ended between us." I rub my hands together and apply the sunscreen to every area of visible skin. I can't stand the stuff, but she's thoughtful for having planned ahead.

"Oh, honey. You truly have no idea, do you?"

83

"Aunt Dee," Henry looks to me then Emily, "Ms. Emily, can I play ball with my friend Scott? I'll be super careful. Promise."

Emily waits for my response, but I nod to her. She's been watching him for the past four days.

"Stay where we can see you. Don't run off chasing the ball," she reminds him.

"Yes, ma'am." He hugs her, then me. "Thanks you."

"He really is a sweetheart." Her laser gaze follows him, running with all his might. "You've done a good job with him."

I ease onto the bench behind us, my eyes glued to my little man. "He's so much like his mother. He has her caretaker heart and gentle spirit. I think he's the one raising me, most days."

She laughs. "He's an old soul for sure, but I think he gets his charm from his father."

The comment throws me off for a moment. Richard saved his charming ways for Lucy. I hardly experience that side of him. I get the lonely widower and adoring father. Charming, I'm sure he saves for work and…

"I wonder if Richard will marry again. Will she love Henry like he deserves? Will she let them remember Lucy, or hide her pictures and change the subject when they speak of her?"

"If she's the woman deserving of their love, she'll accept your sister as a part of their family, help that little boy remember who his mother was."

"Yeah, maybe." My gaze falls further away, past Henry tossing the football. What will I do if that happens? There's no way his new girlfriend-fiancée-wife would want me in a guest room for the rest of their lives. What would I do? Pick up my life as if nothing changed? Could I work in a hospital again and not fear who or what threat is lurking in every dark corner?

Movement has me flashing to Emily, her smile already aimed at me. "What will you do when that happens?"

Wither away and die. "Find a man to make nieces and

nephews for Henry to nurture and guide," I throw out the idea without thinking, half kidding—now, more than half hoping it's true.

"You don't need to *find* a man. He's already here, waiting on you to choose him." She pats my leg. "My Flint is a hard worker, a great doctor, but he's lonely. Something changed in him seven or eight months ago. He no longer finds life as satisfying as he used to." She watches Henry as I can't take my eyes off her.

Eight months ago?

Her gaze flashes to mine. "I think *you* were that *something*."

Nineteen

I T'S BEEN TWO MISERABLE WEEKS SINCE I LEFT DANI IN A heap of tears and agonizing sobs. I never would have left if I thought staying would make a difference. She needs to want me more than her guilt keeps her tied to her sister's life. It doesn't mean it didn't hurt like hell then and now, hence the miserable two weeks.

Mom called every day the first week, giving status updates on how Dani was feeling. I can't say how many times I started to drive over there just to check on her, only to change my mind at the last second, having to trust Mom or Richard would get Dani to the hospital if she needed it.

I thought it was hard to hear how upset Dani was. Turns out, not hearing anything this past week has been even harder. The silence is deafening. The hole in my chest grows with each passing day.

Choose me. Fight for us, my daily mantra.

It seems fast, but really, I've been moving blindly toward her since we met all those months ago.

Me ignoring Nadia, who's been calling incessantly, is further proof of my tie to my little runner. Not many guys could say no to Nadia, but she has even less appeal compared to my girl. Dani may not want me, but that doesn't mean I don't still hold out hope.

The irony is not lost on me. My ex-hookup seems to be holding out hope I'll change my mind about getting serious with her, when, in fact, my heart is all tied up over a woman who won't even consider making a future with me.

Karma is a bitch.

It'll teach me to be more careful who I let in my circle, who I let fill the hole Dani has left behind and may never be filled by her.

"Dr. Heartgrove, Dr. Blake would like a neuro consult. He's in Trauma Bay 3." Nurse Sweet hands me the tablet with Mr. Pierce's chart.

"I'll be right there." I take a moment to review the notes before entering the room.

Dr. Blake glances my way before returning to the patient, listening to his exhalations as the nurse preps an IV. "Dr. Heartgrove, Mr. Pierce fell off his ladder cleaning out his gutters, according to his wife." He stands back, giving me room. "She stepped out to make arrangements for their son after school."

"Has he been unconscious the whole time?" I check his pupils for reaction to light.

"Yes. EMTs said he was unconscious when they arrived, and he didn't stir on the ride over."

"Left pupil is blown; right is reactive. He needs a head CT stat." I stand, folding my arms. "But you knew that."

He smiles. "I suspected. I ordered the scan. You'll give neuro a heads up?"

"Yep. Page me." I step out of the way just as they come to

take him for the scan. I'd bet money to nothing it's an aneurism. If we caught it in time, he has a good chance for a full recovery. But we won't know our next steps until the scans come back.

Nurse Sweet stops me before I get too far. "Dr. Heartgrove, there's a man here to see you. He says it's important but not urgent."

"Did he give a name? Has he been evaluated?" I check my phone to see if I missed a call or text from my office regarding a returning patient coming in through the ER to see me.

She digs in her pocket, handing me a piece of paper. "His name is Richard."

The same time she says his name, I unfold the piece of paper to find one word on it: *Dani.*

Urgency flares. "Where is he?"

"He's in the lounge. I didn't know where else to put him since he's not a patient." Her concern is unwarranted.

"It's fine. Thank you." I rush down the hall, slipping inside the room after an intern exits. "Richard."

Catching him off guard, he nearly spills his coffee. "Flint, Jesus, man."

"Is Dani alright?"

He punches out air and gives a sad smile. "Define *alright.*"

"Richard." I close in. "Is she hurt?" I clarify as if he's truly this obtuse.

"She's fine." He pats my arm as he sits on the couch. "I mean, she's sad as shit. But she's recovering from the accident. She's way better than the last time you saw her."

"Thank God." I sink into the chair across from him.

"That's not why I'm here. I didn't mean to alarm you."

"Did you ask her to move with you?" I ask just as he says, "Do you love her?"

"No."

"Yes," I answer over him. "More than I ever thought possible." Does *he* love her?

"Does *she* know?"

Why is he asking? "I asked her to stay with me, to open a practice with me. Hell, I offered to move and open a practice wherever she ends up."

"That's a business proposition, not a declaration of love," he scoffs. "You seriously expect her to drop everything and stay here with you when you make no promises for the future? She doesn't know how you feel."

"I told her to fight for us. She knows I love her." I jump to my feet and pace to the door and back. Doesn't she? Why wouldn't she?

"No, she doesn't. If you didn't come right out and tell her, offer her a future outside of a working relationship, you can't be upset she didn't dump me and Henry at the chance of a *maybe*. She's not a maybe kind of girl. Not after Lucy. She needs solid ground below her feet. You haven't offered her that."

Damn, I thought I was clear. "She won't choose us over you two. I can't compete with promises made to her sister. She shouldn't have to choose. You have to set her free if she has any hope of having a life of her own."

He scrubs his face. "Damn, I don't want to." He steps away and turns, defeat eating him up. "I didn't realize how much I've relied on her until she couldn't care for Henry after the accident. I lost my heart when Lucy died. Dani was there, making the everyday tasks manageable. It felt like I had a piece of Lucy back—Henry too." He lifts his head, his gaze locking on me. "I need to let her go. For her sake. For Henry's—"

"For you too. Lucy wouldn't want you both holding on to the past and each other, keeping you all from moving forward."

"I thought I was coming here to set you straight." His humorous laugh sinks into my heart.

Looks like we both need to step up and be what she needs.

The one who will let her go. . .

And the other who will catch her.

Twenty

NERVOUS ENERGY ABOUNDS. I'M FLITTING AROUND the house, cleaning because I can't settle into a chair and just wait for Richard to get home. Henry and I ate dinner without him, not that unusual, but tonight, I'd hoped he'd be early so I could get this out of the way. He only has an errand to run, said he wouldn't be too late.

I pause in the living room, taking in Henry building another Lego masterpiece. If I do this, I'll miss so many moments like this with him. I've witnessed many of his firsts, been a part of small and big victories, sickness, and hurts—all the things Lucy has missed: cheering him on, drying his tears, and holding his hand through it all. He's my little man, my sister's son, my *reason* for nearly two years.

Swiping at my tears, I turn away before he notices. My sensitive boy would know something was up, so much like his mother, it hurts.

As I finish the dishes, the garage door motor hums to life. "Your daddy is home," I holler to Henry.

He runs into the kitchen, his socked feet sliding on the floor. He manages to stop seconds before Richard opens the door.

His smile when he sees his boy stabs at my gut. "Henry." He breathes like it's the first substantial breath he's had all day.

"Daddy!" Henry launches at his father as if he hasn't seen him in weeks instead of hours.

They'll be just fine, I try to convince myself.

Richard's eyes meet mine over Henry's head as he stands, carrying his passenger to the island. "It smells good in here."

"It's meatloaf," Henry supplies. "It's so, so good." Everything is *so, so good* according to Henry. He's easy to please.

Drying my hands, I set the towel over the sink's edge. "Would you like some?" I kept it warm assuming he would, but sometimes he eats at the restaurant.

"That'd be great. I'm starving." Richard sets Henry on the floor, drops his wallet, phone, and keys on the counter, and comes around to wash his hands.

Henry rushes over to help me. "Why don't you get your daddy a fork, knife, and napkin and set a space for him at the table?" I direct as I dish up Richard's plate.

"Daddy, can I have ice cream? I can keep you company while you eat." He fiddles with the fork, working to get it just right before turning his hopeful gaze on Richard.

"Only if you're willing to share when I'm done."

Henry turns, his hands on his hips. "Of course, silly." I mean what five-year-old wouldn't share his ice cream? Ha! Not many, I bet.

Richard musses his hair and bends to kiss Henry's head. "You're a good boy."

He'll be an even better man, I've no doubt.

I leave them to man-bond over food and deep discussions of Legos and the world of Harry Potter. I shower, washing off the dust and grime of the day, which is hardly a speck or two. The grime is mainly in my head, digging up feelings involving Lucy's death I'd rather leave buried.

The psychiatrist at my hospital, whom I saw a few times after the shooting, tried to get me to see Lucy's death wasn't my fault.

No one could tell me her blood wasn't on my hands.

She ran out that door at my urging and right into the eye of the storm. Not to mention I was the whole reason she was there in the first place.

"You didn't know," Dr. Charles reasoned. *"You didn't make the shooter pull the trigger. You didn't load his gun, pack extra bullets, drive the ten blocks to the hospital. You didn't know, Dani. You're as much a victim as your sister and all the others."*

"But I lived." Always my answer.

"You did. It's a gift. What are you going to do with it?"

"Take care of my sister's family."

"And what about you? What do you want?" he'd ask.

"What I want is irrelevant." I should have died.

I should have died.

I should have died.

As I stare into my eyes in the mirror, I'm still the same woman I was then, only the damage is not as raw. Now, my heartache is paved with scars and the faltering belief that I had any control over what happened that day.

I didn't cause the shooter to pull the trigger. *There, I said it. Happy, Dr. Charles?*

Of course, he'd say his happiness is not what matters. It's mine.

My happiness? Do I have a right to place my happiness above what Henry and Richard need?

What would Lucy say?

Funny thing is, it's not the first time I've thought that. It's just been a while. When I was a teenager, stuck, and my sister not available, I often thought, "what would she do?" in any given situation. It typically worked.

Stop being a martyr, her voice rings clear as day in my head.

Funny, Sis. I thought I was taking care of your family.

They need to take care of themselves until they're ready to let someone else in. You're my sister, not my sister-wife. You and Richard can't grow in my shadow.

I've always been in your shadow. Nothing new there.

There's no response, except the vision of her giving me the finger before hugging me close. She hated it when I talked about her overshadowing me. I never minded. It felt more like basking in her light than living in the dark.

Then live, for God's sake.

I heard that.

Dressed in yoga pants and a soft tee, I find Richard staring out the kitchen window. "Where's Henry?"

"He's in bed, waiting on you to say goodnight."

"Okay." I turn to leave.

"You can't move with us, Dani," the strain in his voice tugs me around to face him.

Wasn't that supposed to be my line? "Agreed. I was going to talk to you about that after Henry was asleep."

"Yeah? Then it's good we're on the same page. You staying for the doctor?"

"No. I'm staying for me. I need to figure out what I want to be when I grow up," I tease but sadden at the truth of it.

"You can do anything you want, Dani. But I might suggest a doctor's wife."

I laugh, looking around. "You see anyone asking? Besides, I deserve more than being just someone's wife."

He nods then pins me with his sorrowful gaze. "It's nice to be someone's *anything.* Call it what you want. He's waiting on you to choose him."

"What if I choose me?"

"What if choosing him *is* choosing you?" he counters, stepping closer, lightly gripping my arm. "Don't miss out on a chance at happiness. Don't miss a second of letting someone love you. You've survived two major incidents, Dani. I wouldn't want to be in your shoes if you chose to ignore the message God is sending you."

Did I survive being shot and then a train collision for a reason?

Is Flint my reason—or more like, my person?

Richard kisses my cheek as he passes. "Tell Henry goodnight before you leave."

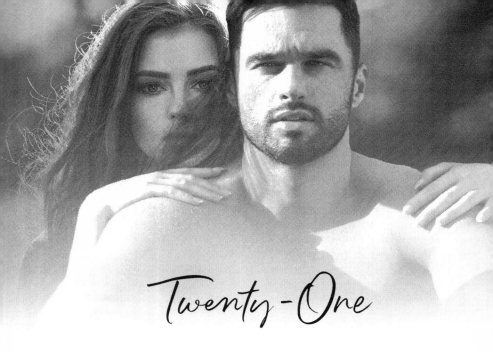

Twenty-One

I'M NOT ONE FOR SURPRISES. I TEXT FLINT TO FIND OUT where he is. He could be working a late shift for all I know. His reply is immediate. He's at home, and he's *looking forward to seeing me.*

Should I stop for flowers, ice cream, whiskey? Should I put a bow on my head? I'm not really sure how this is done. I've never been the pursuer. Will he find it endearing or a turn-off? Flint strikes me as the type who prefers to do the pursuing, but I need to show him how much he matters.

I whip into the next shopping center. Before I can get out, my phone rings.

My heart triple-times it when it's Flint's name on the screen. "Hello?"

"Where are you?" He sounds more excited than concerned.

"I was going to stop—"

"No stops. Don't make me wait any longer. Come to me."

Damn, be still my poor heart. He speaks perfect *Dani,* if anyone ever could.

"Okay," I breathlessly reply.

"The door's open." He hangs up without a goodbye.

I'm thrown back to the first night we met. I followed him home, parking my car behind his in the driveway. I now know he usually parks in the garage, but not that night. That night we were too impatient for such things. We barely made it inside the house before he was inside me.

I shudder from the memory; my nipples harden; my clit tingles. I take a fortifying breath as I park in his driveway, blowing it out and staring at the garage door, working up the courage to step out.

I can do this.

The garage door engages and starts to rise. Two bare feet come into view, then his jean-covered legs.

Oh, how I love faded blue jeans.

Impressive thighs, tapered waist and a V-neck tee are only outdone by his arms crossed over his chest, muscles and veins on formidable display, and the square of his jaw. But it's his eyes that soften his demeanor. Warm, soulful brown eyes heat me up through the windshield between us.

"Get out of the car, Dani," he rasps.

Tingles. Tingles. Tingles.

I turn off the engine and grab my purse and keys. I think I shut the door after I get out, but I'm not entirely certain when he pulls me into his chest. "Took you damn long enough."

I open my mouth to reply, but it's filled with him before I can squeak out more than a gasp. *Ohmygod, I've missed this mouth.*

Missed this man.

Purse and keys dropped, I practically crawl up him like a cat in heat, stealing his breath and moaning my approval when he grasps my ass and grinds against me.

Yes, more of that.

"Are you here to stay?" He feasts on my neck and grabs my breast, squeezing possessively.

"I hope so," I beg as he lays me on the hood of my car, settling over me, between my spread thighs, my legs still wrapped around his back.

"Fuck." He fists my skirt, gathering the material, grinding, and gripping my ass. "Need inside you, my little runner. Tell me *no* or take me deep."

"Not saying *no*."

"Thank fuck." He grabs the front of my dress and rips it open, buttons pinging around us.

"Oh God." That's hot.

He bites my breasts, pulling them free from my lavender bra. "Baby," he sighs as he takes me in, disheveled and laid out for his pleasure. "Missed you, my Dani girl."

He steals my reply with a devouring kiss.

Yes. Yes. Yes.

Between us, he frees himself, shreds my panties, and shoves inside me in a blistering frenzy of need and reckoning.

"Holy—" I arch and claw at him.

"Mine," he chants as he trails kisses along my skin, pinching and twisting my nipples, thrusting hard and demanding.

Fuck. Fuck. Fuck.

Never been so consumed. Burning me up from the inside out. "Harder," I beg. Beg. Beg.

"Don't fucking leave me again," he grates as he stands, grips my hips and nails me to the metal below. "Going to leave a fucking dent in your hood, Dani."

He's going to leave a dent in my soul.

In my heart.

"Please."

"You beg so pretty." He slams into me deep, holding. I

squirm until his thumb finds my needy nub and rubs it merci-lessly. "Come all over my cock. Now." His demand is a trigger, a catalyst.

I erupt, holding on to his arm and the hood, searching for purchase as he shoves deeper and grinds before pulling out to slam in again.

"Flint. Flint. Flint," I cry.

"Fuck, love that." He bends over me, nibbles my ear and whispers, "I love you."

"Ohmyfuckinggod," my cry gets lost as I come again.

He loves me.

He loves me.

He loves me.

I arch off the car. He grips my hips, keeping me from flying off the hood, slamming into me as he covers me with his body, hips drilling, seeking his release. I wrap around him, pulling and pulling. Needing to feel him lose himself inside me, because of me, because of us.

"I love you," I whisper into his neck.

His head pops up, sweat glistening across his furrowed brow. "Say that again."

I capture his face, pepper kisses along his jaw, fighting tears as I repeat, "I love you," across his heated skin.

His war cry as he fills me curls my toes and sends me into another torrential orgasm that has me coming, and coming, and coming until I'm a limp mess on the hood of my car.

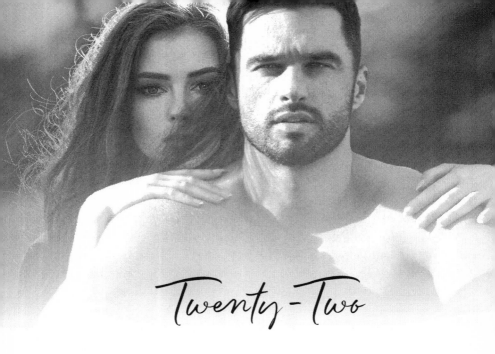

Twenty-Two

"**N**OT DONE FUCKING YOU." I KISS HER NECK AND relish her pussy's tight grip on my cock. But I should take her inside before she comes to her senses and realizes we've just given the neighbors quite a show. I didn't miss the shadow in the window facing my house. Jim has some new jerkoff material, unfortunately.

I sweep her in my arms, dipping low to swipe her purse and keys.

"I'm sorry about your dress." I set her on the kitchen island, whip off my shirt and slide it over her head.

"I'm not." Her soft smile pings in my heart. *She loves me.*

My cock stirs with need to mark and claim what it's been craving for nearly nine months now. "Good." I kiss her nose. "'Cause I'm sure it won't be the last time I rip off your clothes to get inside you."

Her hands clench as she shudders.

Damn, love that. "I love you, Dani," I remind her. "It wasn't a lust-filled admission, in case you're wondering."

She grips my hand, lacing our fingers. "I love you too. I'm sorry it took me a bit to figure my stuff out."

"Is it figured out?" Has she chosen me—chosen *us*?

"Not really, other than I'm not moving. I'd like to try with you if you're open to the idea of there being an *us*."

Her tentativeness on the last line won't do. She needs to understand how much I want an *us*. I kiss her softly before pulling away. "I'll be right back."

I want to kiss the concern off her face, but what I have planned will leave no room for misunderstanding or half-hearted commitments.

Halfway into my closet, I hear the doorbell and backstep. "Can you grab that? I'm expecting an important package."

"Sure," she hollers back.

It's a good handful of minutes later before I'm back in the living room, only to freeze at the sight in front of me. "What the fuck are you doing here?"

Her wicked smile only grows. "Is that any way to greet the mother of your child?"

The fuck? "Come again?"

Nadia stops bouncing and opens her arms to display a small bundle in a flowered cap. "Flint, I'd like you to meet your daughter, Emily Rose."

"You named her after my mother?" My anger is barely contained. Nadia is probably the last woman on earth I'd want to have a child with. Actually, there are no women on earth I want to procreate with except my redheaded temptress—who probably just ran into *this* train wreck...

"It seemed fitting. You have such a great relationship with your mom."

How the fuck does she know that? She's never even met my mom. "What if she's not my kid? Are you going to rename her?"

She gasps.

I ignore her antics. "Where's Dani?" I stalk to the kitchen, already knowing she's not there. The entire house feels cold and empty. She's gone. No doubt Nadia scared her off.

"Honey," she steps closer, placing her hand on my chest, "we have bigger issues to discuss than your latest toy. Though I could dye my hair if you're really into redheads."

I snatch her hand away. "Don't call me *honey*. Don't touch me. In fact, get the fuck out of my house." I point to the door, grab my keys, phone, and wallet. "Follow me." There's only one redhead in my life, and it certainly won't be Nadia with dyed hair.

After I show her out the front door and lock up, I exit to the garage to take my car. I pull up beside her car parked on the street, waiting while she buckles in her baby. "Follow me," I repeat in case she's too shocked by my lack of warmth toward her to remember my decree.

I'm being an ass. My mother would not be proud of me at this moment. But fuck, Nadia scared off my little runner. There is retribution for that.

Nadia wanted *more*. I told her over nine months ago I didn't have more to give. She is beautiful. I'll give her that. But she's a calculating bitch, I found out too late. I don't trust her. I feel sorry for her baby. If the babe turns out to be mine, I'll do what's right. I won't shirk my responsibility. But until then, she and this baby are not welcome in my life.

Nadia's compliant façade slips when I guide her into the hospital's lab. I step inside, leaving her in the waiting room with the command of *sit* and *stay*.

Stepping around the protesting receptionist, I catch sight of Paul. I follow. He stops when he sees me.

"I need a favor."

I helped him with his dad last year when he was diagnosed with a brain tumor. I hooked his dad up with the premier surgeon in the country, sat beside Paul as he waited for his dad to get out of surgery, and then helped interpret the biopsy results. I didn't do it for a favor in return, but I'm not above asking for one now.

Ten minutes later, I'm on the road. Nadia and baby have been deposited in her car with a promise I'll call her when I receive the results.

Dani, my little runner, I'm coming for you. Hold tight, baby.

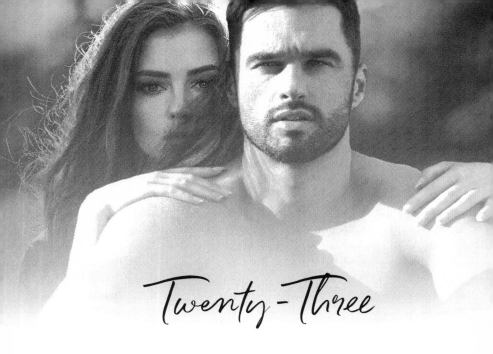

Twenty-Three

P OUNDING ON THE FRONT DOOR HAS ME WIPING AT my face and cracking my bedroom door.

"What are you doing here?" Richard growls.

"I'm here for Dani."

"I don't think so. You couldn't even make it work an hour. You can't—"

"Move before I make you move," Flint growls at Richard.

"There's no way—"

"Dr. Flint, whys you fighting with my daddy?" Henry's sleepy voice trails down the stairs.

I can practically hear the men sigh in defeat. Henry has a way of taking the anger out of your sails.

"I'm sorry I woke you, Henry. And I shouldn't be upset with your father. I'm here for Dani," Flint softening his reply to my little man has more tears leaking free.

"Daddy, don't keep Dr. Flint from Aunt Dee. He loves her. She loves him. If she's not moving with us, we have to makes sure she's taken care of. Dr. Flint will do that, keeps her from being sad like you missing Mommy."

Oh my God. I fall to my knees, my head pressed to the ground. My sweet Henry. All heart and intuition.

"Henry." The anguish in Richard's voice is palpable. "Come here."

"Not until you let Dr. Flint see to our girl," Henry, ever my protector, demands.

"Jesus." Flint concedes to the power of the five-year-old adult in the room.

"Tell me about it," Richard laughs. "You should have met his mother."

"I wish I had, Richard. I truly do."

Shuffling at the door alerts me to company coming my way. I stagger to my feet and step back as Flint comes into view. Any residual anger he holds fades away as he takes in my disastrous state.

"Baby," he breathes as he wraps me in his arms and shuts the door behind him with a soft *click*.

I only cry harder. The sweet men on the other side of that door are no match for the one inside holding me.

He sits in my reading chair, pulling me into his lap, encompassing me in his arms, against his chest. "You've got to stop running from me."

"But that woman."

"No, that's no reason. I had no idea about that situation either. You can't hold it against me. If we're going to be together, you have to stand up for us in the face of trouble. Adversity will come and go, but our love will remain if we hold strong to each other."

I unravel myself from his lap and move across the room. I need space from his all-consuming pull. "You have a child," I point out.

He stands, steps forward and stops a few feet away, sinking his hands into his pockets. "*Maybe* I have a child. We won't know for certain for a few days." He holds out his hand in offering. "I want you no matter what. If the babe turns out to be mine, then I will take care of her, be her father."

With little thought, I lay my hand in his.

Immediately he envelops mine and steps into me. "I will not, under any circumstances, be with her mother. She means nothing to me. It was a purely physical relationship I ended before I met you. She wanted more. I did not—*do* not."

"Where is she now?" *Is she still at his house?*

"I have no idea. I left her at the hospital where we did a rush paternity test. I'll call her when we have the results."

He doesn't want her. "What's her name?"

"The woman or the babe?"

Her brows shoot up. "Oh, God, I didn't consider you'd know the baby's name."

"Nadia named the baby Emily after my mother." He grips me tighter as I gasp and try to pull away. "Just because she named her daughter after my mother doesn't make the babe mine. There are millions of Emilys I did not sire."

"That you know of." I sink into his hold. He's a father. Maybe.

He laces his hand through my hair, tipping my face to his. "I'm pretty sure. I'm thorough. The only woman I've had unprotected sex with is you, my little runner. Nine months ago, and now. It's a game of roulette with you. But I don't need a spin to know I want to be caught by you—with you."

My God, this man and the things he says. "Charmer."

His chuckle is music to my ears, easing the stress in my shoulders. "Tell me you want me even though I might be a father to a babe that's not yours."

That's the easiest question ever. "I want you no matter what."

"Good answer." He kisses my temple and releases me. "Now, where's your overnight bag?"

I point to my closet. "Why?"

He moves with ease and purpose, disappearing inside. "You're coming home with me. My mom will watch Henry tomorrow. We need a day to just be together to seal our bond."

Seal our bond? Sounds otherworldly. "Sounds like heaven."

He stalks toward me, his eyes narrowed and hungry. I stick my ground, taking the impact of our collision as he claims my mouth in a searing kiss. All consuming, rewarding, toe-curling.

"Going to fuck you so good when we get home."

My insides clench, remembering how *good* it was on the hood of my car. "Will we make it inside this time?"

"No promises, my little runner. I've a point to make, a claim to stake, a woman to lock down."

Damn, love the sound of that.

Before we leave, we stop by Henry's room to be sure he's okay and not shaken up by the encounter between Richard and Flint. We find Richard reading him a book.

The minute Henry spots us, he's out of bed and in my arms. "Aunt Dee, are you leaving?"

I hold him a little tighter, keeping him from seeing my looming tears. "I am, but only for a few days. Mrs. Emily will be back to watch you tomorrow. You'll like that, right?"

"Yes, I likes Ms. Emily very much."

Flint kneels beside us, garnering Henry's attention. "I'm sorry for upsetting you earlier. Will you forgive me?"

Henry wraps his little arm around Flint's neck while

keeping the other arm around mine. "I forgives you, Dr. Flint. Just promise to takes care of our girl."

I lose that battle with my tears. My little man can pull them from me faster than anything or anyone else.

Henry studies my tears and smiles. *The little shit.* "Are you done running, Aunt Dee? You gonna let Dr. Flint catch you tonight and all your forevers?"

"Yes, Henry. Consider me caught."

Twenty-Four

"Fuck, baby," I pant behind my little runner, squeezing her ass as I kiss up her back. "Gonna come so hard." She's drawing it out of me, but I'm holding off till she shoots off one more time. I round her clit, driving us closer to the edge.

As soon as she pulled her car into the empty space in my garage, I pushed the button to close the garage and proceeded to relieve us of our clothes. I bent her over the warm hood of my silver Jaguar C-X75 and sank in slow and easy, teasing her, getting her off two times before I picked up the pace.

"Please, Flint," she begs so pretty. "I need to come, or I need to stop, but your slow then fast pace is about to bring me to my knees."

Damn, love the idea of her on her knees, my cock deep, choking her until she gags and tries to take me farther.

"Are you done running from me?" This is not a punishment fuck. I don't believe in those, but she gets hot when I'm demanding and dominating her pleasure.

"Yes. Yes," she sighs, her eyes flashing to mine over her shoulder. "Besides, you keep fucking me like this, I won't be able to walk to the bathroom much less run."

My redheaded temptress, she's going to be so much fun in our bed and out. I kiss the spot behind her ear. "Taking you to bed now, Dani." I pull out on a groan and sweep her in to my arms.

She snuggles in, kissing up my chest to my neck. Her sigh of contentment has me considering letting her sleep instead of continuing what we started in the garage. But once she's spread out on my bed, hips undulating like she needs me as much as I need her, I lose all sanity or remorse over the sleep she's going to lose tonight.

"Fuck," I groan when I'm between her thighs, rutting home over and over.

She wraps around me, arms and legs pulling me in even as I pull out. She moans when I hit that needful place inside, the tip of my cock nudging and loving it just right.

Arching and grinding.

Teasing and taming.

Thrusting and shaking.

She bathes my cock in her warm, wet pleasure seconds before she squeezes me so right. I come as she does, drenching her with my own warm, wet pleasure.

Catching our breaths, I hold her on my chest, half on me, half on the bed. Before she can fall asleep, I carry her to the shower, tucking her into my side while I turn it on and wait for the water to heat, which only takes a moment. Lazy kisses and roaming hands have me growing hard between us.

My girl takes a beat, sucking on my nipples and down my abdomen till she's face to face with my cock. She fists me as best she can, lowering my tip to her lips, and gives a few lashes with her tongue.

"Don't tease," I rasp, ready to drill in deep and hold.

Her eyes flash to mine. "Teasing implies I don't intend on finishing." She flicks her tongue down my shaft, sucking my balls.

"Jesus." I nearly jump out of my skin.

"I've every intention of sucking until you come down my throat."

I capture her cheek in my palm. "Baby." She has no idea how much her giving this means.

She kisses the inside of my wrist. "Hold on, my Knight, and show me how you like it."

My cock disappears as her lips stretch to take me. Shallow pumps with sucking, then deeper with each attempt.

I grip the back of her head, holding her. "Breathe through your nose. Take me deeper." *Fuck, yes.* "Swallow me." *Yes. Yes. Yes.* I groan my pleasure. She only sucks harder. "You keep that up, I won't last."

She practically preens at my praise, her eyes never leaving mine. My beautiful temptress.

Working me hard and deep, I growl as I come, shaking when her throat closes around me, pulling another spasm of cum shooting down her throat. "Fuck, baby."

Breathless, she releases me with a slow slide, falling back on her haunches, catching her breath.

I don't let her rest long. Guiding her off the floor, I lift her up and set her on the curved shelf that sits about waist-high— my waist. I thought it would make for great shower-fucking, but I've never used it. I rarely brought women home, much less showered with any of them.

Her pussy is dripping wet and not from the shower. Slipping my tongue in her mouth, I kiss her silly as I finger-fuck her to a quick orgasm, then drop to my knees. She squeals in shock when I dive tongue-first into her pussy, licking and sucking her juices, fingering her clit as my other hand travels lower.

The thing about my sex-shelf is it has a gap in the middle

where her pussy and ass are open and spread, perfect for fucking either hole. I nearly come from the idea of all the shower sex we're going to have.

I tease her rosebud, slick from her arousal. Her hands fly to my hair as she arches and grinds her hips into my face. My finger breaches her back entrance as I fuck her pussy with my other hand and lap at her clit. As I alternate in and out, sucking and flicking her clit, she jerks from the shock, trying to absorb the pleasure inundating her body. If I had a third hand, I'd be all over those gorgeous tits.

Her incoherent mewls echo in the bathroom. My hips surge forward, fucking the air, so turned on, I might come when she does.

"Oh God, Flint," she screams as she lets go, gushing on my hand, shaking, and curling into herself as best she can, stuck on the shelf like my beautiful plaything. Only she's not that—or not only that. She's going to be my wife and the mother of my children.

Sooner rather than fucking later.

Standing, I pull her from the shelf and onto my cock. She wraps around me, taking me as I fuck her as hard and as fast as I can move my hips. Pressing her into the wall, I free my hands to tease her breasts and love on those tight nips.

Without warning, her pussy grips my cock in a vise-like grip and comes.

"Jesus fucking Christ," I groan as she sucks my orgasm from me with each pump of my hips.

With lazy pumps and tender kisses, we come down from our climactic highs.

"I love you," she whispers into our kiss.

Right then and there I make a promise to myself: I'm going to love her like this every day of my life. Maybe not as many times, but fully present and in awe of her body and heart.

"I love you, Dani. My little redheaded temptress."

I clean us up, quick soap and rinse, dry us off. I carry her to bed, tuck her in, and leave to grab our stuff from the garage, lock up the house. When I return to the bedroom, I find her sitting up waiting.

I hand her a glass of water, which she finishes in one long gulp. *Damn.* "Do you need more?"

"No, I'm good."

Yes. Yes, she is.

"You should be asleep already." I kiss her head as I climb in bed, setting down my glass after finishing my water. Maybe *I* need more. After all, I've no doubt I'll be pumping inside her in a few hours.

"I wanted to wait for you." She half yawns her reply, settling into my side.

Once she's comfortable, I lift her left hand and kiss it, sliding something onto her finger. She sleepily blinks as she looks at it. "What's this?"

I kiss her swollen, abused mouth. "I want you to know how serious I am about us."

She can't fully see the ring in the dark. "It's a promise ring then?"

I roll us till I'm settled over her, my cock hardening at the thought of sliding into heaven so soon. She rubs against me. I don't even think she realizes it. "No. It's an engagement ring. It was my mother's."

"What?" she gasps.

"Marry me, Dani. Be my future, my everything, and let me be yours."

"Oh my God," her whispered exclamation is punctuated by her slipping her legs around me as if she thinks I might try to escape.

The only place I'm going is inside her as many times as humanly possible, for the rest of our lives. "Say, *yes*, baby."

"Yes! Oh, Flint, yes. Yes. Yes."

Damn, I thought I loved her *yeses* during sex. But these right here top any *yes*, past or present.

I claim her mouth, wanting to go easy but knowing I can never hold back with her. She deserves all of my desire and pleasure.

When she's squirming below me, one swift surge, and I'm sliding home on a deep groan, eating up her moans, and feeding her my tongue and cock in equal measure.

"Forever," she moans into our darkened bedroom.

"And ever, Dani." My little runner, my redheaded temptress.

The End

Can't get enough? Want to know what's next for Flint and Dani?
Keep reading for their Epilogue and a chance to get exclusive BONUS Scenes for newsletter subscribers.
https://dl.bookfunnel.com/wpp7ibtnnk

Don't forget to check out all the books in the Doctors of Eastport General series.
https://geni.us/DoctorsofEastport

I'm so excited to announce my involvement in an amazing charity anthology, Heroes with Heat and Heart, benefitting Grassroots Wildland Firefighters organization.
My contribution is Wildflower. What happens when a firefighter has a crush on the shy, free-spirited flower shop owner? Click here to find out!
http://Books2read.com/HeroeswHHV2

If you're a fan of alphaholes and sports romances, then meet the men of my Black Ops MMA Series. They're tough, determined, and sometimes too alpha for their own good. NO MERCY is Book 1 in the series. Gabriel "No Mercy" Stone fell hard for his best friend's woman. To hide his feelings, he ignored her and treated her like dirt. But when things go south with her boyfriend, Gabriel is there to pick up the pieces. When it comes to protecting his Angel, he has no mercy.
NO MERCY - smarturl.it/NoMercy_Amz

Are best friend's sister, friends to lovers, or second chance romances more your style? Then check out my Until You series. Book 1, Until You Set Me Free, is a heart-wrenching romance about a millionaire in the making and his best friend's younger sister. Joseph is everything Samantha is afraid to want, yet she's never wanted to be noticed so badly in her life. Samantha shouldn't even be on Joseph's radar, and yet she is from the day she walks in the room, making him want what's not his to take.
Until You Set Me Free - smarturl.it/UYSMF_Amz

This is a dream for me to be able to share my love of writing with you.
If you liked this book, please consider leaving a review on Amazon and/or on Goodreads.

Personal recommendations to your friends and loved ones are a great compliment too.
Please share, follow, join my newsletter, and help spread the word—let everyone know how much you love Flint and Dani.
dmckdavis.com/subscribe

Epilogue

THE SIGHT OF RICHARD AND HENRY DRIVING AWAY, the moving van following behind, is too hard for words. I know it's the right move, but it doesn't make it any less painful.

"It'll be okay, baby. We'll see them this weekend." Flint hugs me close, kissing my head. "They're only a few hours away, and it's only a handful of days. Mom will be there to help them get settled, give you a chance to relax and unpack your things."

Not that I've left his place since we got married a week ago by the hospital chaplain in front of Richard, Henry, Emily, and a few of Flint's friends and co-workers. But now that Richard and Henry have moved out, I'm fully moved into Flint's house—just not unpacked.

He swipes at my tears, kissing my cheeks. "I know it's hard. I'm sorry."

I've been sad for a week, knowing this day was coming. My sweet man offered again to move too and open a practice there. It's a cleaner break for us to remain here. Richard and Henry need distance from me, from my availability to do and be what they need at the drop of a hat. And I need to find what *I* love again—besides the man next to me.

Buckled up, Flint pulls onto the road, heading home. "Aren't we stopping by the new office?"

He squeezes my hand. "I thought I might drop you home and then run over for a few minutes."

"If it's only a few minutes, there's no reason not to go now." He doesn't need to coddle me, but I sure appreciate that he does.

"You sure?" He kisses my hand, still holding it tight. "I don't mind dropping you home."

"Honestly, I'd rather be with you." Wherever he is, is where I want to be.

His lightning-in-a-bottle smile is instantaneous. "I love that you do."

We've moved quickly, yet it feels right for us, like we started dating all those months ago. Officially, we've only been together a few months, married a week. We're still learning to navigate, ease our way in the ebb and flow of our love. I've never lived with anyone before, and neither has Flint. What we have is uniquely ours, yet still new and growing. I guess you could say I lived with two guys: Richard and Henry. But that's inherently different. I was more like the live-in nanny. No matter how much I loved them or they me, I still felt like a visitor in their home.

I'm not a visitor with Flint. We share a home; every room is mine to explore and redecorate to *my heart's content,* according to him. I'm not quite up to redecorating. We'll see how this semester goes. While Flint is opening a new joint practice with a colleague, merging with an established practice, and moving to a new location that's being renovated—hence today's visit—I'm starting school next week to become a nurse practitioner.

The hope is, eventually, I can join Flint's practice, who currently has an NP, but who knows by the time I finish if Flint will even still be there. He could even decide he misses the thrill of hospital emergencies and traumas he's so used to working.

I like to think I'm thrill enough for my knight, who ravages my body like he's starving and I'm the only meal in town. I don't mind a bit. I particularly love the way he watches me when he thinks nobody is paying attention. The raw love and visceral want in his eyes are enough to make me weak in the knees and clamoring to climb my sexy doctor.

The stop at his new office doesn't take long. Progress is going well. It's going to be a great change for him. He'll only be working four days a week and on call one week a month. Afterwards, we swing by the grocery store to pick up a few items. While he's browsing the wine, I run to the pharmacy, meeting him at the checkout.

His smile zings straight to my girly parts. I sigh into his embrace as he pulls me in for a heated closed-mouth kiss. *Swoon.* Even being domestic is sexy as hell with my man.

Once home, he unloads the groceries, ordering me to relax and find a movie while he cooks. I putter off, not minding him fixing us lunch one bit. I head to our room to use my little pharmacy purchase.

Besides being sad over Richard and Henry's move and missing sleep for all the sex my man lays on me, day and night, I've been unusually rundown. I haven't had a period since the train wreck. I've written it off as a side effect of the trauma and my body healing, but I'm starting to think it's not that—or not *just* that.

Nervously, I pad back into the kitten, one hand behind my back. "Dr. Heartgrove, I have a medical question I need your assistance with."

He quirks a brow at me over his shoulder. "Is that so?" His gaze eats me up, starting at my feet and burning brighter as he catches on my breasts before locking on my face. "I don't think *horny temptress* is a medical condition, exactly." He turns off the stove and rests against the counter. "But I'll see what I can do." He holds out his hand, calling me to him.

I step closer, but it's not my hand I place in his. "How would you interpret these test results, Doctor?"

His eyes linger on mine for a moment longer before he stares at his hand. He visibly swallows with a tight jaw, his gaze burning a hole in the pregnancy test stick.

My heart pounds even louder in my ears. *Please say something.*

"Dani, baby, is this a joke?" he rasps, his voice tight with emotions. Only I'm not sure if it's happy emotions, as he fists the pregnancy test and lifts his eyes to mine.

"I'm sorry. I guess I messed up on taking my pills after the train—"

"Why are you apologizing?" He steps into me, tipping my chin, capturing my lips in a soft, gentle kiss. "Did you think I'd be mad?"

"I hoped not." *I prayed not.*

We haven't really talked about kids in regard to timing, just that we both wanted them at some point. But if the glistening joy in his eyes is any indication, he's not mad at all.

"Are you happy?" A single tear slides down my cheek. *Please, please, please be happy.*

In a flash I'm off my feet and spinning in his arms. "Dani, my beautiful redheaded temptress, I'm ecstatic."

My relief is consumed by his mouth as he fills me with his joy, surrounds me with this love, and ignites a future filled with children and glorious chaos.

He sets me down, bracketing my face with his hands, our noses nearly touching. "Visions of getting you pregnant have flashed in my head from the first time I was inside you." His smile grows, lighting up his entirely too handsome face. "If you want my medical opinion, we need to fuck even more to be sure it sticks."

My giggle is contagious as he joins me, picking me up and setting me on the island where he steps between my legs. Our laughing wanes as he grows serious, gripping my hips. "Thank you for choosing me. For making me a father for the first time, *for real.*"

Newsflash: the paternity tests came back negative. He's not Nadia's baby daddy.

He kisses my nose. "You're the only one I want to make babies with. I hope you're ready, my little runner. I plan on filling this house with little redheaded babies."

My laugh is pure happiness, abating the worry and sadness that have riddled my life since losing Lucy. I'll always miss her. I'll always look out for and worry over Richard and Henry. But this man, right here, has given me a second chance. I survived two devastating incidents and a wannabe homewrecker. I may not find the cure for cancer or end global warming, but my reason for living is looking me right in the face, and I couldn't be happier about it.

I slip out of his grasp, pressing against his chest as I back up. "There's just one thing." My smile drops as my hand falls to my side.

His brow furrows with concern. "What is it, baby?" He steps forward as I take a step back.

"You have to catch me first!" I pivot on the wood floors and dash out of the kitchen, barely avoiding his grasp on my shirt.

He's hot on my heels. "You can count on it, my little runner. I will always catch you."

My stride falters on his last words. Knocked off balance by my rising emotions, he catches me just as I'm about to slide into our bedroom.

"Gotcha," he whispers into my neck as he lifts me off my

feet and strides into our room. "I will always catch you, Dani." His heartfelt promise ripples across my skin.

Catch me he does, over and over, until we can't move, until my body is limp and well loved, until he's ready to catch me again, until we are old and gray, and watching our grandchildren play at our feet.

I was caught by a doctor—a neurologist—who doesn't know a thing about the heart except how to love the hell out of mine.

Want More Flint and Dani?
Sign up for my Newsletter at
dl.bookfunnel.com/wpp7ibtnnk
and receive a free BONUS SCENE!

Author's Note

I fell hard for Dr. Flint Heartgrove. He wooed me just as he
wooed his little runner.
We all deserve a man who will catch us when we run in fear,
waiting until we're ready for *more*.

If you loved Flint and Dani's story, please consider leaving a
review on Amazon and/or on Goodreads.

Turn the page to read more novels from the *Doctors of Eastport
General* series.

About
THE DOCTORS OF EASTPORT GENERAL SERIES

I hope you enjoyed my book, **Doctor Heartbreak**, which is part of the shared world *Doctors of Eastport General*.
https://geni.us/DEGEbook

Would you like to read all of them? Find them on Kindle Unlimited.

Come on in and meet the ER Physicians, Surgeons, Specialists, Residents, and patients that occupy the rooms and halls of the largest hospital on the coast of Rhode Island. We hope you are ready to fall in love with all the sexy stories that take place inside the walls of Eastport General Hospital.

Doctor Heartbreak by D.M. Davis
Doctor Feelgood by Amy Stephens
Doctor D's Orderly Affair by CA King
Doctor Trouble by E.M. Shue
Doctor Temptation by Syd Ryan
Dueling Doctors by DC Renee
Doctor Sexy by TL Mayhew
Doctor Fix-It by Mel Walker
Doctor One of a Kind by Anjelica Grace
Doctor Casanova by Emma Nichole
Dirty Doctor by Amanda Richardson
Doctor All Nighter by Adora Crooks
Doctor Desire by S.L. Sterling

Acknowledgments

If you're reading this, then you are one of the people I want to thank. Thank you for picking up my book, reading my words, and making it not only to the end but to the acknowledgments. Every section, word, thought that goes into my books is meant for you. So, thank you!

To my sweet family that supports me endlessly. Thank you a million times over.

Thank you to my DIVAs for being an important part of my life. Your support and love of my books and writing journey means more than you can ever know.

To all my author friends and the community at large, thank you for your kinship, support, and comradery.

Thank you to my editors, Tamara and Krista, and my PA, Ashley, for making me look like I know what I'm doing.

And last, but definitely not least, to the readers, I thank you for buying my books, reading my stories, and coming back for more. It still amazes me I get to do this for a living, and you are the reason why. I am blessed because of you.
Don't stop. Keep reading! And don't forget to leave a review.

Blessings, Dana

About the Author

D.M. Davis is a Contemporary and New Adult Romance Author.

She is a Texas native, wife, and mother. Her background is Project Management, technical writing, and application development. D.M. has been a lifelong reader and wrote poetry in her early life, but has found her true passion in writing about love and the intricate relationships between men and women.

She writes of broken hearts and second chances, of dreamers looking for more than they have and daring to reach for it.

D.M. believes it is never too late to make a change in your own life, to become the person you always wanted to be, but were afraid you were not worth the effort.

You are worth it. Take a chance on you. You never know what's possible if you don't try. Believe in yourself as you believe in others, and see what life has to offer.

Please visit her website, https://dmckdavis.com, for more details, and keep in touch by signing up for her newsletter, and joining her on Facebook, Instagram, Twitter, and Tiktok.

Additional Books by
D.M. DAVIS

UNTIL YOU SERIES
Book 1 - Until You Set Me Free
Book 2 - Until You Are Mine
Book 3 - Until You Say I Do
Book 3.5 - Until You eBook Boxset
Book 4 – Until You Believe
Book 5 – Until You Forgive
Book 6 – Until You Save Me

FINDING GRACE SERIES
Book 1 - The Road to Redemption
Book 2 – The Price of Atonement

BLACK OPS MMA SERIES
Book 1 -No Mercy
Book 2 - Rowdy
Book 3 - Captain
Book 4 - Cowboy

STANDALONES
Warm Me Softly
Doctor Heartbreak
Heroes with Heat and Heart 2: A Charity Anthology

Join My Reader Group

www.facebook.com/groups/dmdavisreadergroup

Stalk Me

VVisit www.dmckdavis.com for more details about my books.

Keep in touch by signing up for my Newsletter.

Connect on social media:
Facebook: www.facebook.com/dmdavisauthor
Instagram: www.instagram.com/dmdavisauthor
Tiktok: www.tiktok.com/@dmdavisauthor
Twitter: twitter.com/dmdavisauthor
Reader's Group: www.facebook.com/groups/
dmdavisreadergroup

Follow me:
BookBub: www.bookbub.com/authors/d-m-davis
Goodreads: www.goodreads.com/dmckdavis